"Go home, Landis. That's an order."

"We're not at work [barcode] around."

"Watch me."

A muscle clicked in his jaw. "Don't shut me out."

"If you won't leave, I will." She pushed past him.

His arm sprang out to stop her. When she tried to go around it, he pulled her in, wrapping his arm around her. Her back rested snugly against his chest and his chin braced the top of her head. "Kate, listen a minute. I can—"

"No, you can't. You can't do anything to help me. You can't fix it. Now let me go!"

With equal reluctance and frustration, he did. She stared him down. "Don't ever do that again."

He marched off, leaving her confused and upset. She had wanted him to leave her alone, so why did she ache to rush back into his arms and stay there forever?

She didn't need this, this growing dependency on people.

Especially not him.

CHERYL WYATT

An R.N. turned stay-at-home mom and wife, Cheryl delights in the stolen moments God gives her to write action- and faith-driven romance. She stays active in her church and in her laundry room. She's convinced that having been born on a naval base on Valentine's Day, she was destined to write military romance. A native of San Diego, California, Cheryl currently resides in beautiful, rustic southern Illinois, but she has also enjoyed living in New Mexico and Oklahoma. Cheryl loves hearing from readers. You are invited to contact her at Cheryl@CherylWyatt.com or P.O. Box 2955, Carbondale, IL 62902-2955. Visit her on the web at www.CherylWyatt.com and sign up for her newsletter if you'd like updates on new releases, events and other fun stuff.

The Nurse's
Secret Suitor

Cheryl Wyatt

HARLEQUIN® LOVE INSPIRED®

Recycling programs
for this product may
not exist in your area.

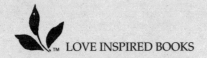

™ LOVE INSPIRED BOOKS

ISBN-13: 978-0-373-87844-4

THE NURSE'S SECRET SUITOR

Printed in U.S.A.

Every good and perfect gift is from above,
coming down from the Father of the heavenly lights,
who does not change like shifting shadows.
—*James* 1:17

Dedication:

To Granny Nellie. There is no one else like you and I love you with my whole heart. You are a one-of-a-kind inspiration. It's easy to see why so many people look to you, and up to you.

Acknowledgments:

My Facebook Reader Brigade, thank you for input on this story. You made it an incredible joy to write. I especially loved your ideas romanticizing the Golden Terrace. Readers rock!

Cara Putman and Sally Shupe, thank you for beta reading this book. I love and appreciate you and your eagle-eye editing. Your friendship is a blessing.

Elizabeth Mazer, what can I say? You are an editorial whiz and I feel fortunate to work with you and hear your fun ideas. Your revision notes make me cackle, grin and best of all, strive to grow. Thank you for putting up with my mischievous humor, "ly" adverb addiction, my tendency to make up nonexistent words, and for enduring my comma confusion. I would cringe if one of my books ever hit a shelf without first being sifted by editorial brilliance. Thankful for you.

Kristi Alexander, you are my hero(ine) for offering the idea to use *Lois and Clark*'s Dean Cain as inspiration for Caleb. I can't wait to read acknowledgments in your books. Believe.

Andie and Aaron Grube, your beautiful masquerade wedding inspired the theme in this book.

Chapter One

Decorated military veteran turned civilian trauma nurse Kate Dalton was known for keeping a cool head under fire. But she'd never faced anything like this.

Here she was, back in the United States, biting back bile and terror as strong as any she'd experienced overseas. When she was in a combat situation, she was braced and prepared for things to go wrong. Here at home, her guard was down. Ten minutes earlier, she'd been enjoying the reception at her friends' masquerade-themed marriage ball. But then the text message arrived.

Phone clutched like a pinless grenade, Kate strode from the wedding reception room to the nearest exit. There. Patio. Best way out. *If* she could get there before hurling blissfully consumed cake.

Regal-hued LED lights danced over her sapphire costume and skin tanned by a three-year deployment under Middle Eastern sun. She probably looked striking— if you didn't notice the tension in her shoulders or the frown on her face.

"Breathe, Dalton, that's an order. You can't fall apart. Especially not where everyone you know can see you.

You don't break down. You don't give in to fear. That's *not* who you are."

Despite her drill-sergeant self-talk, Kate's thumb quivered as it scrolled again over Mom's frustratingly cryptic text.

I'm afraid I have some upsetting news. Call me when you've got time to talk.

Unable to wait, Kate had found a quiet corner of the room and called immediately, but Mom was too distraught to talk. Mom never cried. Something was really wrong. Worse, Dad wasn't answering his personal or military phones.

Terrible scenarios raced through her head. Had something happened to her father? Or to her grandfather, who was scheduled for surgery? She knew the procedure was risky already—her career-military grandfather had ruined his lungs inhaling so much military jet fuel over the years. Had there been another complication? Or maybe her parents had bad medical news of their own. Cancer, heart disease…the possibilities went on and on.

Kate couldn't breathe. Her chest tightened, eyes burned. She rushed out a side door hoping no one saw. She couldn't be around people right now, not until she composed herself. In a secluded corner of a low-lit garden patio, she hid under an ornamental fuchsia tree. Heaving fresh Southern Illinois air, she redialed her mother's number.

An answering click, then sniffles sounded. Kate's jaw clenched. "I'm not getting off this phone till you tell me what's going on. Don't make me leave my good friends' wedding to drag it out of you."

"The wedding! I forgot, Kate. I shouldn't have texted you."

"Did something happen to Dad?" He was a deployed war general, sure, but he hadn't been near danger, had he?

"No. Your dad is safe. It's…honey, it's us."

"What's 'us' mean?" Kate paced. "Me and you? You and Dad?"

"Your dad and I. I didn't want to tell you by phone, but I fly out in the morning for Grandpa's hip recovery. That'll keep me out of touch for days, and I don't want you hearing secondhand. Kate, I need to tell you, your dad and I are divorcing."

"Div—" Kate choked on the last word she expected to hear. *Surely Mom is kidding. Right?* Her mind couldn't wrap around it.

"Kate, Grandma's calling in, probably with a surgery update on Grandpa. We'll talk later, okay? I love you." *Click.*

Teeth grinding, Kate redialed Dad, stat.

"Hello?"

Finally! "Dad?" Kate hated that her voice broke in front of her five-star military hero dad. "Please tell me it's not true."

A deep sigh. "I'm sorry. She served me papers today."

Kate's voice and composure broke. "Daddy, why?"

"Your mom can't handle me overseas all the time. She waited to break the news until she was sure. Kate, are you okay?"

"Not with this. She texted me while I was at a *wedding.*"

"Mitch, your surgeon friend, right? He's one of the ones who founded Eagle Point Trauma Center, isn't he? I remember now. Kate, sorry about the poor timing. With her dad so ill, your mom probably wasn't thinking. Neither am I."

"Clearly. You both aren't thinking. How can you

flippantly throw thirty years of marriage away? Our *family*? And to do it now, when we might be losing Grandpa. Daddy, don't let—"

A presence stirred behind her, and Kate froze. "Gotta go," she barked out, suddenly eager to end the conversation as quickly as possible. "I'll call later, okay?" The last thing Kate wanted was to ruin the festive mood of Lauren and Mitch's wedding by letting one of the guests overhear her having a breakdown. Or let anyone see this crack in her tough-girl image. She never cried. Ever. Not even in the worst combat scenarios overseas or trauma cases here.

Kate flicked a tear but others followed. "Nice night out," she called to the tall shadow over her shoulder. She pretended to gaze at brilliant stars glittering against a raven sky to keep from turning and letting whoever was there see her tears.

No answer—not out loud. Instead, the figure moved; a strong hand weighted her shoulder and turned her around. Heady masculine cologne mingled with pleasant garden scents. Kate tucked her chin to hide red-rimmed eyes, but a leather-gloved finger lifted her face.

Oh, *my.* The most gorgeous, mysterious man stood before her. What she could see of his masked face seemed carved from exquisite stone. His eyes, etched in ebony and concern, were so piercing they arrested her breath. His impressive height strained her neck as her eyes skimmed a firm jaw and sensual mouth and a muscular build that showed serious dedication to fitness.

Silent as a sniper, he removed her fancy feather mask and dabbed her eyes with a blue camouflage-patterned kerchief, the item odd and out of place with his all-black Zorro-type ensemble.

"Thank you." She hated how her warbling voice revealed how she was falling apart. What did the masked intruder want, anyway? "May I help you?"

Dark eyes bored into hers, so intense she startled backward. Embarrassed by her reaction, she opened her mouth to apologize and found herself rambling instead. "I must look raccoonish with mascara running down my face. I didn't even bother to buy the waterproof kind—I wasn't expecting to cry. Not that I'm not happy for Mitch and Lauren, it's just…I don't cry." She let out a brittle laugh. "Except for now. My parents just informed me they're divorcing after a lifetime together." Her voice fractured as the words, spoken aloud, made the truth suddenly become a cruel kind of real.

His chiseled face softened, compassion shining out of his eyes as if he really cared about her, cared about her pain. But how could he? He had to be a stranger. She'd helped each costumed guest sign in and knew each name on the list. No one had been conspicuously absent. He must be a wedding crasher. That she didn't know the guy made him seem infinitely safe. He didn't know her, so he wouldn't judge her for breaking down.

As though sensing her thoughts, he shifted his stance and sweetly adopted a listening pose. Kate drew herself up, surprised at the level of relief she felt at being able to say how she really felt to someone she'd likely never see again.

"My friends inside…they all think I'm strong enough to do anything. I served overseas as a trauma nurse in the army. After that, anything should be easy, right?" Tears pressed for release again. "The problem is, people expect me to be some kind of superhero *all the time*." Her voice dragged to a whisper. "How can I let them see me cry like this? Especially here. It's a wedding—

we're supposed to be happy and hopeful and…and all the things I'm not."

His grip strengthened on her shoulder, fingers gently kneading. She wanted to lean into him. So she did. He stood so near, the leather on his jacket cooled her cheek.

"It's not just because of my parents," she admitted in a low voice, barely more than a whisper. "It's me. The truth is, I hate weddings. They make me scared I'll end up alone after all my friends pair off. I look at brides and grooms who seem so in love, so wrapped up in each other, and I know no one's ever made me feel that way. I've never been able to let go and get lost in the moment and the person I'm with. Maybe I'm too practical to ever truly fall in love. I worry so much about not making a mistake that I never take a relationship risk, never *fall* into anything—not even love."

His sustained presence girded her with courage. His gloved hand settled against her back, nearly a hug. Stalwart. That's what he was. Plus a stranger. Which meant she could spill her guts without leaving behind an emotional mess she'd have to clean up, explain away or deny to death later. And something about the night… the moon…the masks…made her embrace being honest, being vulnerable. What could she possibly have to worry about when being in his arms felt so safe?

He responded by drawing even closer. Care ebbed off him in waves, dangerously appealing combined with his handsomeness. It didn't even occur to Kate to protest as he dipped his head and covered her mouth with his in a mesmerizing dance.

He exuded strength, mystery, masculinity and hints of delectable spearmint. His breath, his kiss were so soft. So delicious. Everything else fogged. Stress from her parents' devastating news melted. Her world contracted to the cove of his arms, the core of gentleness driving his kiss and the calming rhythm of his breathing.

He broke contact to press his mouth to her ear and whisper, "Hang in, sweetness. Darkness never defeats the dawn." His voice held a gravelly quality, as if he'd disguised its coffee-rich depth. She tilted her chin up.

Uncertainty flickered in his eyes before his lips found hers again. This kiss felt final. Declarative, like a seal over a covenant. Dizzy and disoriented, Kate swayed. Strong arms braced her up as he pulled her in for a hug that felt more like pure comfort.

Then he bolted.

"Kate?" The voice of her best friend Bri Landis drifted from a doorway. No wonder the bandit had fled. The crasher had sensed company before Kate had, and hadn't wanted to get caught.

After the sensation of being stun-gunned subsided, Kate faced his retreating back. "Wait! Who are you?"

But her bandit had already scaled the eight-foot-tall wood fence, cape flying behind him like a flag, and she lost sight of him.

"Marvelous Masked Intruder, come back," she whispered into the inhospitable night. Bri's voice neared, reeling Kate back to reality. Kate banged her forehead on the fence. Why hadn't she chased him down? Simply put—she couldn't.

He had taken her by such sublime storm and surprise, and that kiss had so incapacitated her, she wondered if she'd imagined it. She put fingers to her lips and tingles there whispered she most certainly hadn't.

Kate couldn't kick the insane urge to find him and spend time with him again. Not only because of the amazing kisses, but also for the way it had felt to have someone she could really *talk* to—someone who would listen without judging and comfort without questioning. All the things none of her friends would imagine she'd ever need and that this stranger had offered automatically. That kind of thing could go to a girl's head. It made her sad to think that the beautiful moment they'd shared would be the only moment they'd ever have.

"Hey!" Bri approached, dressed to the nines in a frilly-winged fairy costume but with a warmly concerned look on her face. "I got worried when I couldn't find you. Everything okay?"

Kate slid onto a nearby bench. "Yes. No. I don't know." Bri was the one person she could talk to about this. Kate thanked God Bri was who He sent.

Bri sat next to her. "What's going on?"

Where to begin? "Well, there was Mom's mysterious text and thirty years thrown away like yesterday's trash, then a man dressed as a bandit in black leather appeared out of nowhere. We talked—well, I talked and he listened. And then…we kissed. He swept me off my feet, really—until he vanished. Jumped the fence when he heard you coming out to find me. Night swallowed the most appealingly compassionate creature who ever lived."

Bri blinked slowly. "Wait, text? What text?"

Kate calmed herself and took time explaining everything from the first text from her mom, to the blue camo handkerchief wiping away her tears, to the kiss that ended with her bandit disappearing over the fence. She only left out the part where she'd confided her fears about never finding love. Bri was currently engaged and blissfully happy—Kate didn't want to make her friend feel bad. That part of her little breakdown could remain a secret between her and her bandit.

"Kate, there's no one remotely dressed like a bandit

here. I took photos of each and every person in their costumes for Mitch and Lauren's memory-book gift."

Kate shrugged. "I know. He had to be a stranger." Kate left out the part where knowing he *was* a stranger made him easy to talk to. It would hurt her best friend's feelings to be told Kate found it easier to pour her heart out to someone she didn't know. "Probably a wedding crasher who heard about the masquerade theme, since he knew enough to show up in costume. Whatever his reasons for being here, he did manage to show up at exactly the right time, when I needed someone to listen to me unload about my family fracturing apart."

Bri nibbled her lip. Kate flinched at what she'd said and the painful memories she might have stirred. If anyone knew what fractured family felt like, Bri Landis did. Her father had been the first to drop out of her life— he'd walked out on the family when Bri was a child. Now he sat incapacitated in a nursing home with all hope of reconciliation gone. Her mom had passed away recently, leaving Bri to tend a run-down family lodge alone. Her brother, Caleb, the only family she had left, was deployed overseas, dedicated to building his military career.

Kate sighed. "I'm sorry, Bri. I shouldn't be melodramatic, in light of all you've been through."

Bri shook her head. "Nonsense. Things are looking up for me. While I desperately miss my geeky gun-toting army-medic brother, I'm freakishly in love and freshly engaged to Eagle Point's most gorgeous anesthesiologist." Bri wiggled her ring-embellished finger, reminding Kate how much there was to be happy about. Yet a twinge of sadness hit Kate instead. *Mom, Dad...*

"I'm also fulfilled being a mother figure to Tia. Though she's only five, you and I both know Ian's daughter is an amazing gift and constant source of joy. And of course her daddy and our wedding plans are equally bright on my horizon."

Bright horizon. Kate recalled the bandit's admonition that darkness never defeats the dawn, as the confidence that usually carried and defined Kate ebbed back. Grandpa could still get better. And her parents' divorce wasn't finalized yet—maybe things could still be fixed. If not, as Bri had reminded her, there was still so much to be thankful for.

Like a moonlit kiss from a handsome stranger.

Kate brushed the thought aside. She'd probably never see the bandit again. He was just someone God sent her way to give comfort she needed at her lowest moment. She'd weathered it, and was ready now to be strong on her own again—as always.

"Speaking of that handsome fiancé of yours, let's go back in before he wonders where you are." Kate rose to her feet.

Bri stood, as well. "Sure you're all right to go back in?"

"Of course." Kate flashed Bri the grin that used to win her the tiara back in her beauty-pageant days. "I'm always all right."

For a second, Bri looked as though she wanted to argue, but with a shrug she let it go, leading the way back into the reception hall. Kate followed her with a quick, confident stride.

And if she paused for a moment before stepping through the door to look back at the spot where she'd last seen her bandit...well then, that was no one's concern but hers.

Bzzzt! Army medic Caleb Landis snatched his phone before it vibrated off the sun-bleached windowsill. Stumbling out of his sleeping bag, he tripped over his bandit costume before finally settling on his feet and checking the phone's display.

Sergeant Asher Stone. Not surprising. Their unit chaplain would be the first to check on Caleb's well-being. The pair had received unexpected temporary leave of duty for exemplary service after extended back-to-back deployments and had left Afghanistan the same day.

"H'lo." Caleb shouldered his phone to his ear as he rolled up the sleeping bag and checked out the window. No sign of anyone outside. Good—that meant his sister hadn't yet noticed that he'd crashed in cabin seven of the family's lodge the previous night without letting her know he was there. He couldn't resist the temptation to surprise her.

"Hey, Landis. Calling to make sure you made it safely in."

"Yeah, after a two-day flight delay back into the States."

Asher whistled. "Wow. Seriously? Did you make it in time for Mitch's wedding?"

"Nope." Caleb turned a bucket upside down and sat on it. "Missed the whole ceremony and the first half of the reception. I didn't even get a chance to congratulate the bride and groom before—" Caleb cleared his throat, blaming early morning fuzzy-headedness for what he'd nearly let slip. "So, um, how was your flight home?"

"Hold up, Landis. Before what?"

"I…ah…ran into someone before I could go into the reception. We talked for a while. And then I…left."

"Left?" Asher repeated. "Without even going in? Must have been some talk. Wait a second, was it *Kate* you talked with?"

Caleb frowned. Asher knew him way too well. "Who said anything about Kate?"

"*You* did, Romeo, for hours at a time after your last stretch visiting Eagle Point. Come on, it's not like you were subtle. Everyone in the unit knew about your insane attraction to Kate, who scarcely knows you exist. But hey, if she talked to you she must know you exist now, right?" Asher chuckled disbelievingly on the other end of the line.

"Well…sort of." Before the previous night, he'd seen the beautiful nurse on only a few occasions. While Kate knew of him through her friendship with Bri, he'd bulked up since his last visit and he was certain she hadn't recognized him at the point of the kiss. To complete the costume, he'd worn black contacts, disguising his gunmetal-gray eyes. And he…hadn't been like himself. Yes, he was always spontaneous, so that was nothing new, but he wasn't usually that smooth, that suave. He'd seemed to know exactly what to do to put her at ease, and that was a bizarre and unfamiliar situation for him when it came to a pretty woman. Especially *that* pretty woman.

Kate was Kevlar-strong to the core in a way that demanded respect. She and her family had earned enormous admiration among the military community, and she herself was a living legend. It had thrown him for a loop to see her so brokenhearted. Caleb had only wanted to alleviate the pain that put the tears in her pretty, sapphire-blue eyes.

"Do I want to know?"

"Doubtful. I screwed up last night. Didn't handle the Kate thing well. It wasn't my brightest moment."

He didn't—couldn't—regret the kiss. But he also couldn't help feeling he'd taken advantage of her vulnerability to steal a kiss Kate wouldn't have given him under any other circumstances.

Putting aside the fact that he was pretty sure she really didn't know he was alive, except as Bri's little brother, he also knew from his sister that Kate was only looking for romance with *non*-military men. She was done with the danger of that lifestyle, and wanted a stable man she could count on to be around. Army medics like Caleb need not apply—especially considering his efforts to get accepted into the rangers.

"Anyway, I didn't even get a chance to let my sis know I'm in town for four months. Hopefully she won't be too mad. Maybe she'll forgive me once I tell her I plan to renovate her bunkhouses before I leave and take that load of stress off her."

"Then Bri's wedding before you go back."

Caleb chuckled. "Sure, remind me. I leave a brother-in-arms stateside to watch over my sister and he finagles her into marrying him and adopting his daughter." He liked Ian, though. He treated Bri well and brightened her outlook after losing Mom.

"Hey, you'll have a little niece to spoil." Asher laughed.

"Yeah. I'm gonna buy Tia all the noisy toys." Caleb smiled upon hearing Asher's son, Levi, chatter in the background. It put an empty twinge in Caleb's chest. He'd always wanted a son. But it wasn't like he could pursue a family while training for ranger school. "Levi's glad you're home, I bet."

Asher's silence alerted Caleb this conversation was hard. Asher, an explosives expert as well as the unofficial unit chaplain due to his strong faith and natural, charisma-laden leadership, wasn't easily rattled. Caleb sobered, remembering Asher's recent abandonment by his wife. "He cries over his mom every night," Asher finally said. "His tears are the toughest hurt I've ever had to take."

"Sorry, man. You've got faith, though. You'll get through." Caleb knew what being left by a parent felt like. Not good. Poor little Levi. At least Asher drew strength from God and prayed. Caleb was still too ticked over Mom's death to try.

"So how is Kate, anyway?" Asher's voice held a serious note.

Caleb recalled the agony in Kate's voice when she'd spilled about her parents splitting up. If anyone knew how to pray for Kate, Asher would. "Kate was a mess when I got to her. She'd been crying. Not hard, but hard enough for Kate. She's by far the toughest woman I know, inside and out."

"What was wrong?"

Caleb was confident Asher would do nothing with the sensitive information except pray, but he still wasn't willing to share details. Kate had trusted him with those, and he'd keep them private. "Family stuff. Twisted me up to see her hurting." In fact he'd almost caved and pulled his mask off when he'd spotted the tears reflected in the moonlight. But something took over and he'd just listened. Then he'd held her, then *kissed* her and she never once resisted. Proof that what made her cry had her insides turned upside down.

In truth, Kate Dalton scared him to death. It had nada to do with her third-degree black belt or her prior work as a hand-to-hand combat instructor for special ops personnel.

What scared him about Kate was that she made him think about things like home and family. Things he wanted, yes, but not yet. He had a plan, a goal—and something about Kate made him want to throw it all aside. Caleb shook his head, reminding himself to keep focused. He had to stay on track. He had to achieve his goals. He had to prove himself, once and for all. There'd be time for love and romance only when he was done.

Besides, he knew he wasn't what she was looking for, either, and the last thing either of them needed was another hurdle or heartbreak. Clearly, they weren't compatible as a couple—their dreams weren't conducive to that. Still, the thought of the pain in her eyes the previous night made him ache. No, romance wasn't on the table, but they could be friends during his time home, couldn't they? She'd looked like she needed a friend.

"She needed a shoulder to cry on—and my shoulder happened to be handy. It was nothing more than that."

That Asher grew silent on the line again gave Caleb pause. "Levi's suspiciously quiet. I better go investigate."

"Keep in touch, all right?" Caleb really looked up to Asher, particularly for his unabashed reliance on God. Not that he'd admit it. Yet.

"Gotta keep up with the Kate saga. Later, man."

Caleb ended the call, chuckling. Not once had Asher preached. Just listened like a friend. Maybe Caleb could be that for Kate—a friend in time of need. Sure, he'd have to battle some attraction, but Caleb was used to overcoming obstacles. Her appeal would fade and they'd enjoy an uncomplicated friendship while he was in town.

Caleb set his phone on the sink. He caught sight of the bag harboring his disguise—and Kate's mask. He picked it up. He hadn't meant to take it with him. He just…hadn't wanted to let it go. He ran a thumb over the silken edge. It reminded him of the feel of Kate's lips. Elation vied for shame at the underhanded way he'd stolen a kiss when Kate had been too vulnerable to push him away.

Guilt prodded Caleb. The diamonds dusting the edge of the mask's cat eye looked real. It was probably valuable. He needed to give her stuff back.

Now he had a new dilemma. How to let Bri know he was here without cluing Kate in to his arrival. He couldn't let her make the connection between his arrival and the bandit's. Not yet, anyway. If she knew what he'd done, she'd be furious with him for not unmasking himself the night before.

Later, when she'd had some time and distance from that night, he'd tell her the truth. She'd understand that he hadn't meant to trick her. He'd only wanted to be there for her—as a friend. Nothing less.

Nothing more.

Chapter Two

Like anesthesia, it had worn off.

For the first day after the reception, the memory of her bandit and his words about darkness and dawn had been enough to keep Kate's head held high. She'd been certain everything would somehow work out with her parents, and her grandfather's health, and the whole mess her family had become.

But now, the following day, some of that certainty had started slipping away. "I always thought my family was stable, you know?" Kate jogged around ruts with Bri on their favorite outdoor running trail. "Of course, that's not to say there were never any problems...."

"Like when you came here?" Bri suggested as she caught up with Kate. To their left, scenic Eagle Point Lake scrolled by. To their right, lush emerald foliage scented the air.

"Exactly. Dad and Grandpa weren't happy I ended my military service, against their wishes. But look where their careers got them. One disabled, one about to get divorced. If Dad had ever stepped back from his career and focused on his marriage—made home and family a priority the way I wanted to when I left the service—

then maybe he wouldn't be getting a divorce today. And Grandpa's surgery wouldn't be nearly so risky if his service hadn't ruined his lungs. Why can't they see that I was right to leave it behind when I did?"

Bri's countenance reflected compassion. "You were a terrific military nurse, Kate, but you're doing great work here, too. No one has the right to blame you for wanting to go where you could be happy and have the life you want."

"Yes, the *civilian* life. Thanks for understanding." Lifting her face, Kate inhaled fresh air and absorbed the breathtaking scenery. "I love Eagle Point. It's serene and quiet and quaint—everything that I want out of life."

Sunlight glittered off the lake, highlighting impressive Southern Illinois bluffs and hiking trails. "In all my military moves, it's the first time I've felt truly at home. I never want to leave it."

"Especially since I'm here," Bri teased.

Kate laughed. "One more lap around the lake?"

Bri groaned. "You just enjoy punishing my leg muscles."

In truth, running and the scenery calmed Kate, took her mind off things and caused her heart to reach and yearn for its creator. Maybe He'd help save her parents' marriage.

"Ah, well. We're working off the massive amounts of cake we consumed at Lauren and Mitch's wedding," Bri conceded with a laugh.

"You're next." Kate winked and refocused her breathing.

Bri smiled brightly. "Three months. I feel bad my wedding plans are interfering with us hanging out."

"It's okay. It's a season. I'll adjust. Things will go back to normal soon." Yet even as Kate said it, she had the horrible sensation things never would. Not as far as her family went. But the last thing she wanted to do was put a damper on Bri's joy. "I've got a few new things to keep me busy. Keep my mind off my parents' junk." Kate kept her tone light and expression upbeat.

"Like what? Finding a certain bandit?" Bri winked.

Kate laughed. "Well, if he tracked me down again, I wouldn't say no.... But seriously, I know I'm not likely to see him again. No, I've got some other projects lined up that should keep my summer pretty busy."

Bri's cheeks flushed with exertion so Kate slowed the pace as she continued to explain. "Mitch hit me up to be on the fund-raising committee for Eagle Point Trauma Center expansion projects. First item on our agenda is Lauren's grandpa's first annual storybook ball."

"I heard Lem was considering that but didn't know it was a go yet." Bri slowed as they neared the end of the run.

"Yep." Kate glanced to the side. "You realize proceeds from the ball go to your bunkhouses, right?"

As Kate knew she would, Bri balked. "That's not necessary."

"Quit being tough on yourself when people reach out to help. Everyone knows you and Caleb almost lost the lodge, and everyone wants to see you make a success of it, instead. It benefits the community. Plus, you're remodeling two bunkhouses for family members of trauma victims, which will be a terrific boon for our trauma center." Kate swigged from her monkey-themed water bottle.

Bri nibbled her lip and sighed. "I guess it will be helpful for the town overall. Housing and hotel options are virtually nonexistent in Eagle Point."

"Precisely why I'm glad you're letting me move into

the first of your cabins that passes inspection." Kate paced her breathing. "Mitch has been merciful about the distance I live from EPTC, but the fact is, when I'm on call and we get a bad case, I need to be less than fifteen minutes away. My apartment is twenty."

"The cabins should all pass inspection next month."

"Great. Because crashing in EPTC's nurse call room is not conducive to rest." Kate sighed as her phone buzzed on one hip, her beeper on the other. "Ian." She grimaced at Bri. "Since your fiancé is blowing up my phone instead of yours, I'm assuming we have an incoming trauma." Kate hit the answer key.

Ian came on the line. "Kate? All is well here, but you have a rather interesting delivery at the nurses' station."

"My favorite Chicago-style pizza with anchovies?"

"Hardly. You should probably just come get it."

Kate didn't miss the probing curiosity in Dr. Ian Shupe's voice. Head anesthesiologist on their trauma team, he was like a protective older brother to Kate.

"Fine. I'll be right there." Kate disconnected and nodded to the trauma center. "Apparently I have some sort of special delivery. Ian wouldn't say what it is. Mind coming with to see?"

"I'd be glad to." Bri grinned and toweled sweat off. "Especially since it means I get a glimpse of my man in scrubs."

Kate shook her head and sauntered toward the glass-and-brick structure across the parking lot and next door to Bri's main lodge. Inside EPTC, Kate's coworkers parted like the Red Sea when she reached the desk.

Kate's sneakers screeched on the polished floor. On the desktop ledge, her elaborate sapphire-feather mask sat neatly atop a parchment envelope.

Oh, my! He didn't. Kate gulped. Ignoring the stares

and curious grins, she forced her hands to move slowly as she reached for the items. "Who brought this?"

Ian leaned in. "That's what we were all wondering."

Kate straightened. "You mean no one saw him?"

Ian's grin exploded. "Aha! So it *is* a him?"

"That's not your business." Giving up all pretense of nonchalance, Kate snatched the items, scowled at her coworkers and marched to her nurse's call room.

"Kate, wait. Ian was kidding." Bri caught up, giggling.

Kate whirled once they were safely behind closed doors. "How did he manage to get this stuff in here without anyone seeing him? We need security cameras installed at that desk."

Bri bit her lip but a grin burst through. "Open it!"

Kate sighed and fingered the gold scrolling font on the envelope's front.

For Sweet Kate.

"He knows my name," Kate breathed. Then removing her hand from her chest, she added, "Not that I care." She cleared her throat and scowled, especially when Bri responded with a curious look.

Kate peeled the envelope's seal, wondering if she was imagining hints of his cologne on the parchment or the rush of happiness she felt as she began to read.

Dearest Kate.

Although I hate to give you back the means to hide any of your beauty away, I did feel honor bound to return this mask. Please forgive me for stealing it—and for the other thing I stole out on the patio. It was a theft I should probably regret more than I do. May you find it in your heart to forgive me. Nonetheless, you outshone every star that glittered in our sky. Sapphire suits you. You looked

*stunning. It was my honor to be able to share that
moonlit moment with you. Most important, don't
forget to remember the dawn.*
Fondly,
BB

Bri leaned over her arm. "BB? Who is BB?"

Kate could scarcely concentrate on Bri's question. Her hands, always steady in any circumstance, were shaking. She handed Bri the note and walked numbly to the sofa, struggling to come to terms with why she felt so moved by his words. She was a beauty-pageant queen—it was no surprise when men thought she was attractive.

But maybe that was what had her so surprised.

Usually when people admired her it was when she was at her best—winning a pageant, saving a life in trauma, being a leader in whatever way people around her needed her to be. Her bandit, though, had seen her at her tear-stained worst…and he still seemed to think it had been an honor to be with her.

"Benevolent Bandit!" Kate said in a sudden burst of revelation. "That must be what BB stands for."

"Or maybe Beloved Bandit?" Bri teased as she joined Kate on the couch and handed her back the note.

Kate's cheeks flushed as she reread the letter, and something unexpected fluttered in her heart. Kate mentally ordered it to stand down. The last thing she needed was to get excited over a fly-by-night guy. "Benevolent," she repeated firmly, "because he was there for me when I needed him. But nothing more is going to come of it. Certainly not love. This bandit—though charming—had 'inability to commit' etched all over him. That he ran off proves he's a flight risk. That's not what I'm looking for in a relationship. I want someone stable. Not someone who parades around crashing weddings and kissing strangers senseless under cover of moonlight."

"His kiss made you senseless?" Bri smirked.

Kate groaned. "Only for one hundredth of a second. Look, if I wanted unstable, I'd re-up in the military. I'm grateful for what he did the other night and for returning the mask and leaving me this note, but that's where it ends." Kate's fingertips brushed his admonition to remember the dawn. "Being around him gave me a peace I can't explain. Like his words added ammo to my faith and left me certain everything's going to end up okay." Kate folded the paper and tucked it back into the envelope. "He feels like a new friend…except for the unfortunate fact I have no clue who he is or where he lives." Kate laughed at the irony.

"I think you're right not to look for anything serious with this guy, especially since he didn't even bother to share his name. However…don't write him off yet. Maybe he'll show up again. That wouldn't be a bad thing, would it?"

"What are you saying?"

"Things like sweet notes and mysterious gestures might make a nice distraction for you."

"You mean, getting my mind off my parents' divorce."

Bri slid an arm around her. "I can't get out of my mind the brilliant glow on your face as you described him wiping away your tears. Crazy kiss aside, I think a benevolent bandit might be what you need in life at the moment. Someone to occupy your thoughts and cheer you up."

Kate patted Bri's cheek. "You cheer me up."

"But I'm swamped and it's bound to worsen with wedding plans, Tia and bunkhouse renovations."

"It'll work out. I'll help, too." Kate flexed her arms.

"You may need to go help your mom with your grandpa. If he continues to go downhill after his hip fracture…"

"I know. If Grandpa gets worse, I'll head to Chicago to be with my family. The last thing I want to contend with is regret. You taught me that. But Mom's a nurse, too. She can handle it for now."

"Then promise me something."

Kate groaned. "That statement from you never ends well for me." But she raised a resigned eyebrow. "But shoot, anyway."

"Give me your word that if—*if*—this BB guy continues to send you notes and stuff, that you'll stop resisting and enjoy it."

"You're impossible, Bri. But since I love you and your incurable optimism, I'll agree." Bri smiled kindheartedly yet eyed the clock in a fidget that reminded Kate Tia was coming home from her aunt's in St. Louis. "Let's walk you back. I forgot Tia's on her way home."

The two women escaped out EPTC's side door and walked the parking lot in companionable silence, to Kate's relief. "What do you have planned today?" she asked as they approached Bri's gorgeous caramel-and-golden-hued lodge.

"Ian's bringing kitchen paraphernalia so he, Tia and I can make cupcakes. That child is a baking fanatic, like Caleb."

Kate saw sadness cross Bri's face. Heard the telltale break in her voice. "I know you miss your brother. When does his tour of duty end?"

"Not anytime soon. He applied for ranger school." She pulled out her phone as they went in. "I'm kinda worried about him. He hasn't called in a few days. I hope he's not facing something dangerous."

The time had come to bite the bullet. Caleb had to let Bri—and by extension, Kate—know he was in town. He rolled up his sleeping bag after the third night in the empty cabin and glanced at the diminished pile of leftover war rations that he'd been living on, along with stale canteen water, for the past three days. Stalling was no longer an option.

True, he still didn't know how he was going to tell either Kate or Bri about his interlude as the masked patio bandit…but if days of mulling over that question hadn't given him an answer yet, he wasn't likely to find one. He'd have to wing it.

He dialed Bri's cell phone. She answered on the first ring.

"Caleb! Finally. I was so worried! How *are* you?"

"I'm good." *Mostly.* He steeled himself against homesickness rustling through him like the breeze as he walked familiar landmarks toward the lodge kitchen. He knew Bri and her fiancé, Ian, baked goodies on Saturdays with Ian's daughter, whom Bri was adopting. There they were. His heart swelled seeing the warm family scene through the window. After the rough year they'd had losing Mom, he loved to see his sister smiling. Excitement welled over having a little niece to spoil. "I have a surprise for you."

"What's that?" Bri helped Tia stir some kind of dough.

"Look outside the yard window to your left." Caleb smiled.

Bri blinked over, saw him and dropped her phone. Her

shriek carried all the way outside. Ian looked up sharply as Bri rushed from the lodge and threw herself at Caleb.

"You're home! When did you get here?" Her words muffled over each other as she wept and hugged the stuffing out of him.

"Not long ago." Three days after a yearlong deployment wasn't long, right?

Ian approached with a grin and Bri's pink batter-laden phone, which she'd apparently dropped in the bowl. Ian wiped it then hauled Caleb into a man-hug. "Good to have you back."

Caleb eyed him funnily. "I'll put up with mushy stuff only because we're gonna be family now. Seriously, dude. What up? I ask you to bodyguard my sis and get a brother-in-law out of the deal. Smooth, man, smooth." Caleb laughed, as did Ian.

Caleb knelt when Ian's daughter skipped up. "Hi, princess. You must be Tia." Caleb stuck out his hand but Tia plowed past it and hugged him. What was it with all these huggy people?

"You'll be my new uncle who buys me all the noisy toys!"

Caleb snickered. Ian eyed Caleb with a smirk. Bri planted her hands on her hips. "Is that what Caleb told you, Tia?"

Tia nodded her head proudly. "Yep. *Uncle* Caleb."

Caleb grinned. "Speaking of toys, I have something for you here." He went to dig in his pouch pocket for the frilly doll he'd picked up for her. When he pulled it out, one of his blue camouflage kerchiefs slipped loose and fluttered to the ground.

Bri's eyes snapped right to it. She paled as she slowly looked up to stare at Caleb.

Four disbelieving blinks preceded her stare shifting into a *glare*.

He averted his gaze but felt his sister's acrid gaze as she studied him. Somehow, she knew.

After a minute of chatter from Ian and Tia, Caleb chanced a glance at Bri. She chewed the inside of her cheek and looked worried.

Ian looked from one to the other, obviously picking up on the tension between siblings. "So, Caleb, I bet you're hungry after the long flight. Let's get you fed." Ian motioned them in.

Bri's eyes narrowed. "Yeah, just when *was* your flight in, Caleb?"

He cleared his throat. "The details are sketchy."

"Not for her." Bri shook her head and stomped away.

Ian's forehead crinkled. "What's that about?"

Caleb sighed, knowing he'd deluded himself thinking he'd have a chance to explain his side of the story before his sister found out the truth on her own. "Trust me, you don't want to know."

Once inside, Bri cornered him. "It was you, wasn't it?"

He clenched his jaw, knowing the time had come to face the music. Or, in his case, the firing squad. Wordlessly, he nodded.

"What were you playing at, Caleb?"

"I wasn't playing!" he protested. "I'd just gotten in. I had a costume ready because I'd planned to be in time for the ceremony, but my flight was delayed. I thought I'd be able to at least stop by the reception to congratulate Mitch and Lauren, and then I saw her there, crying…"

"Her parents had informed her, moments before, that they are getting divorced after thirty years of marriage."

Caleb knew that, because Kate had shared it with

him. Bri mentioning it meant Kate's parents were still at odds. Caleb's heart sank. "Poor Kate. I was hoping they'd reconciled."

"Reconciled what?" A voice sounded from the front door.

Kate. Could he convince Bri to keep what he'd done a secret? Doubtful—she was too angry with him. His reckoning had come.

Caleb pinned Bri with his gaze and leaned in. "Let me be the one to tell her. Please."

"Fine."

Caleb sauntered toward Kate like she was a human gallows. Bravery fled. He was certain she'd be upset or disappointed to learn the bandit she'd shared a special moment with was him. It would ruin his chance at being a friend for her. But there was no other option.

Swift motion to his left drew his attention. Bri put a restraining hand on his arm and nibbled her lip like she wasn't so sure now. "On second thought, Caleb, that thing we just discussed?" She sliced a hand across her neck. "Abort mission. I'll explain later."

Kate approached, sweeping silky brown bangs from her eyes with choppy motions. "Wow. Welcome home, Landis. Should I leave? Feels like I walked in on a private conversation. Strange, considering I believe you were discussing *my* parents' divorce when I walked in." Kate sounded aggravated.

Caleb couldn't blame her. No doubt she thought Bri had been oversharing about Kate's private business. He could clear up her confusion in no time at all…so why wasn't Bri letting him?

Bri stepped between Kate and Caleb. "I'm sorry. I should have asked you first before saying anything."

Kate shrugged, flipped hair over her shoulder. "Doesn't

matter. It's only Caleb." She retreated, buddy-buddy with Bri, to the counter, effectively blowing him off.

It's *only* Caleb? So that's where he stood?

He tried to remind himself her dismissal wasn't sup-posed to bother him. After all, he'd spent the past three days thinking about why they wouldn't work together as anything but friends.

Tia skipped from the woodsy forest-critter-themed kitchen where Ian looked occupied cleaning up a bak-ing mess out of earshot. "Miss Kate, can you be my taste tester?"

"Ooh-rah! Cupcakes. My fave!" Kate leaned down to take a bite.

With Kate distracted, Bri dragged Caleb outside onto her gleaming redwood deck. "You don't need to tell her yet."

"Why not?"

"I'm worried about her. She's taking the news about her parents really hard—especially since her grandfa-ther's sick, too. She needs something to cheer her up. You signed your note BB, so she thinks you're a benevo-lent bandit. I think the BB could brighten her days and give her something to look forward to."

Caleb shook his head. "BB meant Bri's Brother. I was planning to tell her the truth—at some point. I didn't want to lie to her. I just wanted…" He'd just wanted to help her. And she wouldn't have accepted help or com-fort from "only Caleb."

Bri clutched his T-shirt. "Please, Caleb. Don't tell her yet. While she may not see or admit it, she actually needs the BB right now. The distraction, and the way you unwittingly made her feel, really helped her get through these past few days. I'm certain of it. Yes, she needs to know the truth, eventually, but not yet. She's devastated enough with life. Let's wait at least until her parents' ordeal calms down."

"I don't know, Bri. You really want me to continue tricking her?"

"You don't have to trick her at all. Just keep being the guy you were on the patio—the one who has made her smile just thinking about him for the past few days. That guy took her mind off her troubles—don't you want to keep doing that for her? I asked God to send help for Kate. She refuses to burden me. God could be using you to keep her from going off the emotional deep end right now."

"You really think keeping the…the Benevolent Bandit around will make such a difference?"

Bri shrugged. "Maybe. Isn't it worth a shot? Kate's dealing with so much right now—she needs something that'll make her happy. On top of all her family issues, they have crucial inspections coming up at the trauma center. She needs her head in the game or they'll lose vital funding."

"EPTC, they hurting?"

"No, they've outgrown themselves and need to expand."

"They hiring? I was hoping to work part-time while I'm helping you with renovations and stuff. I'm here four months."

"I'm so glad. I'm sure they could use you at the center, especially since Mitch is gone for two months on a combined honeymoon-mission trip with Lauren. They'd already booked their flights when they received word of the inspection timeline moving up."

"I'm happy to help if I can."

Bri's face lit up, and Caleb felt a sudden rush of foreboding. That smile from his sister always meant trouble.

"If you really mean that, then you could do me a favor and be on the storybook ball fund-raising committee in my place. I don't want to leave them shorthanded, but I've got a lot on my plate right now. Organizing is right up your alley, not mine. Then I can focus on Tia, wedding plans and the lodge."

"Sure. Hook me up with whoever I need to talk to about it."

A smug expression made it clear that he'd fallen right into her trap. "This'll get interesting."

Caleb straightened. "What are you not telling me, sis?"

Her eyes shone. "Kate's on the fund-raising committee, too."

Chapter Three

What was *he* doing here? "You stalking me, Landis?" Kate slid into the only empty chair, which happened to be next to Caleb, at the first storybook ball fund-raiser planning meeting two days later.

Caleb looked up. To his credit, he looked surprised. "Pardon?"

This close, incandescent lighting illuminated the strength of his jaw, the chisel of his cheek, the divot gracing his chin and the nice curve of his mouth. When had he grown so appealing?

Kate settled deeper in her chair and looked away, scolding herself for finding him so. The last thing she needed was attraction to someone destined for the front lines. Too many families—hers included—were ripped apart by war. That wasn't what Kate wanted for herself, when it came to love. "You're like my shadow."

"Whaddaya mean?" For an imposing, well-built military guy, he looked skittish all of a sudden.

"First at Bri's cabin this weekend, and now here at the Eagle Point Civic Center meeting."

Guarded relief settled over his face. "I was at both

places before you got there," he teased in lighthearted tones. "Maybe *you're* stalking *me.*"

Kate was shocked and a little appalled at the way his words made her blush. To hide her face, she became extraordinarily interested in the *Frontline Army* magazine he held. Nostalgia marched through her at the images of military medics tending service members. *Quit it. That's your old life, remember?*

She cleared her throat. "How long are you here?"

"An hour, same as you." He smirked.

"Ha. Always the joker. I meant how long stateside?"

"Four months. I leave after Bri's wedding."

"At least you get to be here for that, before throwing yourself back into d—action." She'd almost said danger.

He didn't need to be reminded.

"Yeah." He cleared his throat and seemed fidgety. Was she making him uncomfortable? Replaying their conversation in her head, she realized she'd probably sounded too accusatory when she sat down. Remorse filled her. She was in a crabby mood, thanks to all the issues—personal and professional—taking up her time, but that was no excuse for being rude to her best friend's hero brother. Especially since he had such a short amount of time to enjoy being home before he was sent off again.

Kate admired his courage, yet feared for his safety. She'd patched up too many gung-ho brave souls just like him. She cared, for Bri's sake of course. Caleb was all the flesh-and-blood family Bri had left.

Keep him safe, Lord.

Maybe Kate could befriend Caleb while he was in town. It would be nice to have someone to spend time with, particularly since Bri would be too busy to give either one of them much of her attention. Bri would want that for her brother and, like Bri, the scope of Kate's problems tended to dwindle when she focused on someone else's issues.

She stuck out her hand. "Let's start over. Friends?"

He took her hand, then glanced to her face before looking away. He was acting so strange. Guilty, almost. Looking back, he nodded. "I'd like that."

They fell silent as the meeting was called to order. Kate tried to pay attention as the monotone mayor droned on, but found herself distracted by the solid, shy man beside her.

Lem Bates, Lauren's grandfather, approached them after the initial information was presented. "Caleb and Kate, can you two head up the storybook ball props?"

"Us? As in, together?" Caleb raked a hand over his buzz.

Lem grinned. "You two are the youngest whippersnappers on the committee. Some of the props get heavy after they're built. We could use your physical strength and stamina. Besides, building those props could take long hours. I think you'd work well together."

Caleb flicked a glance her way and back to Lem. "Me, too."

If it didn't bother him, then it wouldn't bother Kate. "Props sound like fun." Her phone bleeped a text from Mom. Kate stilled when she read that Grandpa's vent settings were adjusted as much as they could be. Kate swallowed, realizing he may be nearing a point when there'd be nothing else the doctors could do.

As Kate readied to text Mom back with "Should I come?" she was horrified to find her fingers trembling on the itty keypad. She was also mortified to feel the heat of Caleb's stare on her. She looked up and tried to neutralize her features.

"Everything okay?" He glanced at the phone pointedly.

After debating a second, she tilted the message screen so he could see. "My grandpa's having problems. Could you let Bri know?"

He nodded slowly. "How about you, Kate? Are you okay?"

"I'm fine." She despised the quaver in her voice and the draw of his.

He raised his chin and held her gaze, making her feel her facade was far from effective. He shifted toward her and the text.

Something about the set of his shoulders seemed strikingly familiar all of a sudden. Silly, right? Why, she could count on one hand the number of times she'd seen him. Must be the sleepless nights spent awake, praying her guts out for Grandpa and her parents, playing tricks on her mind.

She pressed her phone into her purse, wishing she could tuck uncertainty away, too. She shrugged, trying to project calm. "With Grandpa, it is what it is."

Concern in Caleb's eyes only intensified. Kate rose from the table both to escape his overwhelming empathy and to visit the ladies' room.

Once at the door, she peered back, glad to see Caleb now occupied with scrolling and poking through his smartphone instead of scanning the pointless, dumb emotions pulling at her heart and playing out over her face, making her feel incredibly exposed and weak.

Lem, watching them both more shrewdly than Kate

was comfortable with, seemed to sense her escalating discomfort and moved on to the next two people on the committee.

Caleb didn't feel a bit sorry for what he was about to do.

Kate might have said she was fine, but the tremors taking over her eyelids and fingertips spoke of high stress levels.

Her mouth might have uttered *it is what it is,* but he knew good and well "it" was breaking her apart. He'd be happy to be her shield, but she wasn't ready to let him as Caleb. What about BB?

While Kate composed herself in the bathroom, he texted his sister and asked her to bring the note he'd tentatively written Kate as BB. He'd planned to leave it on her car after her next on-call night shift at the trauma center. But he'd use it now.

Via return text, Bri agreed to sneak it onto Kate's car. Several moments later, a second text from Bri confirmed the delivery had been planted on the Jeep, parked where no one could see the benevolent transaction.

The words he'd written ran through his mind and he hoped they'd bring healing from uncertainty and worry.

Hello again, Sunshine,
Hoping you remember that not even the darkest
nights can overtake the day. Do you know your
eyes shine like the sun when you smile? Shine
often.
BB

Once the meeting concluded, Caleb and Kate stuck around to discuss the next steps of their project and walked out together. Crossing the parking lot, he peered up the sidewalk for an eatery. Everything he'd known was gone, and not a lot of new joints had popped up to take their places. Sad. But it only highlighted how important to the town the work could be that Kate, Mitch, Ian and Bri were doing.

Folks were depending on the trauma center and their lodge to dig the town out of financial ruin.

Too bad he wouldn't be here to see it built back to the bustle it'd had when he and Bri were little. Nostalgia and homesickness hit, nearly making him wish he didn't have to leave in four months. Caleb squelched the thought and squared his shoulders.

He'd never make ranger school with that kind of waver.

"I'm starving," he said, fighting to overcome the shyness that made him hesitate to talk to her. "Where's a good place to eat around here now?"

Kate studied him carefully then gestured across the street. "One block down there's a joint called Sully's. They have to-die-for chili burgers." She peered around. "Where's your car?"

Caleb chewed the inside of his cheek and feigned interest in the ant colony invading fresh-cut grass near the sidewalk.

Kate turned a one-eighty. "Seriously, where's your ride?"

Gut churning, Caleb kicked the brick steps. Cleared his throat. "Uh, right there."

Kate stared at the bright purple bicycle and stepped over to brush a hand along the white wicker basket in front. Her finger trailed along big neon plastic flowers plastered to it.

"It's Bri's. I sold my truck to help pay for lodge repairs." Caleb's ears flamed. Kate would forever razz him about riding a girlie bike. It couldn't have saved his ego a little by being a mountain bike or a masculine color, either.

Kate slowly turned. Respect rather than mischief twinkled from her eyes. "You mean you rode this? Straight through town where anyone could see it?"

He shrugged. Looked away. "I said I'd help out with the committee, and I wasn't going to go back on my word. Pride comes last. Plus, I didn't wanna take Bri's car. She has Tia."

Kate was next to him in a flash, lifting his face much the same way he'd lifted hers that night on the patio.

"Caleb Landis, you are more of a man than any truck-toting male around. I don't know of a single other guy who'd have the guts to ride that through town." She released his face but the soft sensation that her fingers left remained. "Still, it'll be dark when we get done eating. So let's put your bike in my Jeep and I'll drive you home. And, for future reference, call me for rides."

He wasn't about to argue with that. Not only would it save him some face over the girlie bike, it would afford him a few more moments with her to find out how her parents and granddad were doing.

They started down the sidewalk when Kate detoured down the alley toward her Jeep with Caleb following, leading his bike. His palms moistened. He hadn't wanted her to find the BB note in his presence. Caleb lagged back.

She turned. "Aren't you coming?"

She flashed a grin of such warmth it made him not only walk into a decorative, steel light pole, but grab it and say, "Excuse me."

Kate snickered enough it started him laughing, too.

Felt good. Furthermore, she looked burdenless, all incapacitated with laughter. So he was glad she did, even at his expense. He just wished he could get past feeling as klutzy as an elephant on ice skates around her. The only time it had gone away was when he'd been BB.

At her car, she initially passed the windshield and then arced backward. Her cheeks tinged red as she slipped the note from her wipers.

Caleb angled away, trying his best to look simultaneously patient, oblivious and bored. In reality, his heart thumped like a war drum.

Despite his best intentions, Caleb could not keep from watching Kate's quiet yet profound reaction as she read. Her shoulders relaxed and the twin dimples that occasionally accompanied her megawatt smiles peeked through.

Bri was right. The note lifted Kate's burden. For now.

He saw the moment she realized that the first note he'd left at EPTC with her mask wasn't going to be a one-time thing—that her bandit would continue to reach out to her. And as long as he lived, he'd never forget the look of tangible relief. Her chin wobbled precariously. She covered it with her hand before he could see for more than an instant, but he didn't have to see to know.

The bandit's kind gesture almost moved her to tears.

He looked away, partly to provide her emotions a cove of privacy but mostly because if he didn't, he'd rush over there and do something more stupid than walk into a light pole. Like hug her.

The note was enough. It would *have* to be enough.

If he was closer to God and sure he'd be heard, he'd beg God to let it be so.

A few moments later, as if aware of his scrutiny, she snapped to attention, tucked the note into her snakeskin handbag and schooled her features. Nevertheless, she seemed stronger now, taller and more peaceful. As they would say in military speak—*at ease.*

Caleb bit back a thankful smile and experienced profound relief that Kate didn't seem to suspect he'd written the note or that his sister had delivered it secretly.

"Your bike can go here," Kate said as she popped open the back. "And once it's stowed away, can you grab that bag?" Kate nodded to the military rucksack in her backseat as she hefted a camouflage duffel bag. She must have used both overseas because they were well-worn and military.

What was she doing with the bags? He restrained his curiosity, figuring that soon enough he'd be able to see for himself.

"Think you'll ever go back?" Caleb asked as they marched with the bags back through the alley toward the main street.

"To Sully's? I go there all the time. I love it."

"I meant the military. Heard you were top-notch."

Her face hardened. "I have no interest in that anymore. I served my time." She smiled stiffly up at him, which almost made him trip over himself as he paused to let her pass. "I do have an interest in downing a Sully's Super Chili Burger, however." She grabbed his shirt and steered him there.

Bossy little thing. Of course, she'd been a drill sergeant.

Once inside the diner, she advanced as though she owned the place and set the duffel inside the owner's office door. She gestured for Caleb to do the same with the rucksack he carried. Reading the confusion on his face, she answered his silent question.

"Sully's owner reminds me of my grandpa. They were

war vets and served at the same time. Sully lost all his military stuff in a house fire. All he has left is what's in here." She gestured at war memorabilia on the diner walls. "I figure this stuff means more to him than to me."

Alarm trickled through Caleb as well as a sense that she was making a rash decision. "You're really sure about getting rid of these?"

"I am." She lifted her chin, face dared him to talk her out of it. "That's my old life. I don't want reminders of it." She raked harsh eyes over his T-shirt's army triathlon emblem.

He could see that Kate's walls were granite-hard and fortress-high now, unlike the vulnerability she'd displayed in the garden at Mitch's wedding. If she'd only open up like that to BB, then that was yet another reason why the masquerade needed to continue.

Caleb glanced through Sully's office at Kate's hard-earned and respectably decorated past, abandoned and crumpled in two heaping bags on the shoe-scuffed floor, and squelched the urge to tell her she might regret giving it all up and walking away. After all, did he *really* know her well enough to make that call?

You know her better than she realizes, down to the satiny feel of her lips and how her chin quivers when she cries, something whispered inside him. Probably his unwieldy conscience.

Would Kate be livid once she found out he was BB? Probably. But if BB made her life better now, the wrath was worth it. Right?

"You look like something's on your mind." Expressive eyes watched him intently as he motioned her into a booth. Hair spilled over her shoulders as she scooted in. She'd grown her dark brown, cropped military hair out to luxurious lengths.

He almost commented on it but clamped his mouth shut, sat and stared ahead. Some things were better left unsaid. "It'll work itself out." He slid a menu her way.

She leaned in. "Sometimes talking about it helps."

A laugh choked out of him. "Trust me, not this time."

The waitress brought ice water. Kate sipped hers like a regal princess. He resisted the urge to guzzle his. Manners were in order. She was, after all, a lady. "Thanks, Caleb."

"For?"

She shrugged. "Friendship. Hanging out. For getting me."

"I get you?"

She grinned. "Yeah. I think you do."

Caleb sliced a piece of nut-dusted French bread for her.

"I could use a friend," she added. "Bri's strapped with wedding plans. I'm not the type who thrives alone. I get into too much trouble." Mischief brightened her gorgeous eyes.

He laughed and tried not to dwell on how astonishingly pretty she was when she smiled. "Somehow, I can believe that."

"See? I told you that you get me. It's proof we're going to be great friends."

The waitress, a pale-skinned waif with coal-black hair, came back and took their orders, then left them alone again. "I'm glad we're both comfortable with just being friends," Kate continued. "Otherwise, people in town might try to fix us up."

Caleb struggled not to choke on his water. "R-really?"

Kate nodded. "Yeah, besides our waitress and a few others, there aren't many people our age in town, so everyone seems to think a newly arrived single man must be my Prince Charming."

"But that's not what you think," he said, even though he already knew the answer.

"Nope. I'm not interested in you romantically. It's nothing personal!" she hastened to assure him. "You seem like a great guy, and I'm glad we're going to be friends. But you're military all the way, and that's not what I'm looking for."

He nodded. "Fair enough. I'll only be around for a few months anyway, and then hopefully it's off to ranger school, so it's not like I have time for romance, either." He thought he saw a flash of disappointment cross her face, but it was gone before he could be sure.

"So we'll make the most of the months as friends. After all, we'll be spending a lot of time together with fund-raiser meetings and the work we'll do together to ready props. Plus, Ian texted Mitch and informed him you applied at EPTC part-time as a surgery tech. Mitch called Ian first thing this morning."

Caleb perked up. "You think I got the job?"

Kate grinned. "I mess with his and Mitch's to-do list all the time. You're top of the list for him to call for an interview. Well, after SpongeBob."

He chuckled. "You wrote that in, or what?"

She shrugged. "You know from being a military medic that humor is what gets us through hard nights and heavy case loads."

He nodded slowly, enjoying having that military and medical connection with her. Maybe being friends with her while keeping the secret from her wouldn't be awkward after all. Sure, he wasn't as smooth as he'd been as BB, but they were still getting along.

"We're bound to run into each other at the trauma

center and in surgery," she continued. "Plus, Bri and Ian invite me for dinner once a week, and I assume, since Bri can't stand to leave anyone out and you're her beloved brother, you'll be there."

Caleb coughed. He'd swallowed a piece of ice whole when she said *beloved brother*. Okay, yeah. Totally awkward here. After he recovered, Caleb leaned in. "Good point. Look, you don't have to try so hard to convince me to be friends, Kate. That's not like you, anyway." He grinned. "I'm fine being friends with you. To friendship?" he suggested, lifting his water glass in a toast.

"To friendship," she agreed, clinking her glass against his.

Chapter Four

Kate had been right about one thing—Caleb had been told in no uncertain terms that he was absolutely required to attend weekly dinners with his sister, Ian, Tia and Kate. And that's where he found himself the next week's Thursday evening, grinning as he watched his soon-to-be-niece give the doll he'd brought her a "ride" on the back of her puppy, Mistletoe.

The cotton-on-ginger-colored dog pranced in a regal circle, but the entire back half of the dog wagged as he stopped and peered up. Caleb, looking down at him, was met with soulful brown eyes, a playful bearing, a happy pant and breath only a puppy could get away with. His expectant, hopeful expression matched Tia's mischievous one.

"It's a toss-up as to which of you is cuter."

Tia's increasingly comical antics caused him to chuckle. He'd about decided that someday having a little girl wouldn't be half bad. Caleb glanced over to see Kate watching them with an approving smile as she chopped apples in the kitchen for a fruit salad. He grinned back at her and winked.

For a guy with limited experience dealing with kids,

his babysitting gig seemed to be going pretty well. Sure, Bri and Ian were there to step in if anything went wrong, but they were so wrapped up in each other, he wasn't sure they'd notice if he and Tia set the kitchen on fire. Things had been so busy for both of them lately that he knew the engaged couple needed time together.

Two beepers sounded. Bri shrank in disappointment. Ian and Kate sobered and pulled out their chiming cell phones. Caleb's grin faded as he stood, instinctually knowing Ian's creasing forehead meant something bad was headed to the trauma center. Tia quieted, and the dog seemed to sense her unease because he moved closer.

"I'm sorry, babe. I gotta go." Ian kissed Bri's forehead, hugged Tia then followed Kate, already out the door. Every nerve ending in Caleb strained and ached to go with him. He'd been doing combat medicine for so long it felt strange to sit back and watch an emergency go by without running headlong to help.

Bri sighed. "He's been on call four days in a row. With Mitch and Lauren away, and Dr. Lockhart, the anesthesiologist, taking some personal time, the trauma center is short staffed. He really has no choice but to be there," Bri said, as if to convince herself it was all right and temporary.

But Caleb could tell she missed Ian and he her. The center had erupted with traumas this week and the engaged pair barely saw each other in the two weeks since Caleb had been here. Even then, they'd only waved in passing when Ian came to pick up Tia. No wonder Bri's renovations had fallen behind. She couldn't take a child into a construction zone. Caleb grew even more thankful he'd received military leave. His sister and her cabins needed him.

Caleb felt heartsick at her disappointment over not

being able to cook for her fiancé and not getting to enjoy the meal, much less the evening, with Ian. Caleb rose from the rug to meet her in the kitchen but she bravely waved him back down and approached the carpet, instead.

"What did you decide to name her, Tia?" Bri asked in a light tone and brushed a hand down the doll's long, flaxen hair.

"Calebina, of course." Tia's bright smile sent unfamiliar feelings through Caleb. "After my awesome, amazing uncle, who rescued her from the clutches and brought her to me from a land far, far away."

Actually, it had been the discount store down the street at the local airport, but he wasn't about to wipe the adoration off the kid's endearingly cute face, framed in a riot of brown curls and bedazzled with freckles. Though he knelt on the rug beside her, he felt easily three feet taller. Especially since she really looked convinced he'd rescued the doll from "the clutches." Clutches of what, he had no idea. The twinkle in Tia's eyes and the joy in Bri's as she peered lovingly at Tia made the worst *clutch* he could imagine not seem to matter.

"Calebina." Bri smiled and winked at Caleb. "Of course. I should have guessed." The love between Bri and Tia was tangible. Caleb could see how much happiness the two brought each other. They'd both been through hard times, but those experiences had brought them together. Thankfulness shifted something small but vital inside him. Maybe it was a bit of the grudge he'd been holding against God?

"What clutches did Caleb rescue her from, Tia?" Bri asked.

"The clutches of death! Death by broccoli," Tia announced dramatically. Commotion across at EPTC's lot cut their laughter short. Whipping rotor blades beckoned Caleb to the window where he watched two helicopters land outside the trauma center. Twin ambulances also pulled up. Staff scurried to them. Caleb grew concerned when stress mounted on the faces rushing around. He thrummed to go help, but he hadn't exactly been hired yet. Could he—should he—go? Should he not? He shuffled foot to foot in an effort not to bolt there.

Bri's phone rang. The second Bri said, "Yes, he's here," Caleb skied across the waxed wood floor and grabbed the phone.

"Hey, Landis, if you're up for it, we could use a hand over here." Ian's voice strained through the cacophony of background noise.

Adrenaline, gratitude and readiness buzzed through his veins. "Be right over." Caleb hugged Bri, scrubbed a quick hand through Tia's hair before shoving his shoes on and hopping out the door, while trying not to trip over the rug-of-a-dog. He jumped the steps and sprinted to the trauma center. Ian waved him past staff and occupied gurneys near the first set of surgical doors.

"Scrub up. The surgeon needs someone else in there, stat."

At Ian's directive, Caleb found and changed into scrubs, washed his hands at the sterile sink, donned a hat and mask and backed through the O.R. doors into complete chaos—raised voices, code alarms and a slick floor that wasn't supposed to be covered in crimson. He eyed the man's blue lips and nail beds. *Dear God...* Caleb surprised himself by praying. *This guy's toast if You don't step in.*

"Grab another unit," Kate directed as he rushed over. A nurse gloved him up, then Caleb exchanged one bag

of near-empty blood for a full one resting amid a pile of
others on a stainless-steel cart.

Realizing her mind could trigger a different masked
encounter, he put his back to her as soon as he could,
prepping a second IV. When Caleb turned back to the
group and the emergency still going south on the table,
he secured a second IV line without having to be told,
which drew nods of approval from Kate and Ian.

Caleb looked around for code meds in an effort to
crash-orient himself to the room setup and supplies
they'd need. It was a struggle to locate everything, since
he'd never set foot inside this room before. He piled meds
and supplies on the table and started quickly ripping
open package after package of whatever they needed.

Moments later, Kate nodded to him, then down. He
swiftly took over compressions, which freed her to grab
supplies he'd have a longer time finding. He appreciated
her intuition and rapid actions.

When the vascular surgeon suggested they call the
code, Kate flat-out refused to give up. Over the next
hour Caleb was filled with respect as he watched the
team battle to save the man's life.

Kate not only multitasked but drilled order after order
to the other nurses and staff, who looked to her skill as
much as to the doctors for guidance. Even the vascular
surgeon cast admiring glances her way as the patient
actually improved and was transferred.

Another patient followed, and while this one was
less critical, a third patient tanked, which took most
of the staff out of the room, leaving Kate to man the
care of the third patient and the code of a fourth. Caleb
watched once more as her quick actions and stream of
split-second decisions saved two lives in a row.

Hours later, after the accident victims were stabilized

and the next crew took over, Ian motioned Caleb into the doctors' lounge.

Ian extended a phone to Caleb. "Mitch wants a word with you."

Caleb smiled, knowing Ian's smirk meant he was about to be offered a job. Indeed, Mitch thanked Caleb and confirmed his employment before ending the call so Mitch could, as he put it, "return his attention to his beautiful wife."

Ian perched on the desk and Caleb thought it odd that his smirk hadn't retracted. "Mitch told me to have Kate show you the ropes in terms of in-house policy, procedure, et cetera. You gonna be okay with shadowing her, Landis?"

The statement seemed loaded, somehow. Too much like a baited trap for Caleb's ease. Ian watched Caleb the way Asher did when studying unclear overseas maps of potential explosive-device hot spots.

Caleb stood his ground, poker face in place. "If you have somethin' to say to me, Shupe, let's get it on the table now."

Ian's smirk stretched into a full-fledged grin. Had Bri shared about the bandit with him? Or was Ian's perceptive radar picking up stuff on its own? Like Caleb's innate attraction to Kate that had flared as he'd watched her in action?

Regardless, Caleb couldn't get out of his mind Kate's words that night on the patio. She'd confided to the bandit how much it weighed on her when people expected her to be invincible *all the time*.

He saw it firsthand tonight. He now fully realized the intense pressure Kate felt to live up to others' perceptions of her. How could he ease her burden? Or at least ease others' galactic expectations of her?

People truly did depend on her. She was the best at what she did and exemplary in emergency care, even in the midst of her own private-life trauma. She didn't buckle, bend, weaken, break or even flinch tonight in the face of some of the worst injuries he imagined she or her team had ever seen.

He admired her. Big-time.

If respect was what Ian was sensing, so be it. Kate had more than earned it.

Yet Ian was acting as if he knew something more than that. Caleb was reminded of the way Bri had bragged about Ian's ability to see inside people and realize things about them even before they did.

Ian play-slugged Caleb's shoulder. "All I have to say, Landis, is keep up the good work. On *all* fronts."

With that, Ian strode out, chuckling.

Leaving Caleb alone to vacillate between confusion and determination not to ponder what Ian might have meant.

"I have a proposition for you," Kate said to Caleb. Her on-call shift had just ended, and when she'd had a second to think about the rest of her day, an idea had occurred to her. As she walked to the employee parking area, she hoped Caleb could help her put it into action.

She hadn't seen the man since they'd worked the traumas together a few nights prior. They had made a great team. Surgically speaking, of course.

She knew he'd been officially hired, but unfortunately, unlike her, Caleb actually had a couple days off. Bri mentioned he'd left town for a military training operation with some of the Refuge Pararescue Jumpers—PJs for short. Kate knew he'd be back today, hence her phone call. She was hoping he could help her work out her plan to get Ian and Bri some much-needed face time.

"Yeah?" he answered. "What's that?"

She opened her mouth to answer, but then her eyes caught on a paper on her Jeep's windshield, flapping in the rare summer breeze. From BB? Her heart jumped, even as she tried to tell herself it was probably just an advertising flyer. "Hold on. Someone stuck a piece of paper on my— Holy smokes! He did it again." Kate stared at the homemade greeting card under her windshield wiper blade.

Once again, BB had left something on her Jeep and sneaked away without getting caught. Probably because Kate hadn't alerted anyone to watch. She hadn't wanted to admit to anyone how much she was hoping for another gesture from her secretive friend. To tell about the bandit would be admitting the needy, emotional train wreck she was right now. She struggled to get herself on track, even with prayer. So, to Kate, the benevolent bandit was a Godsend for all.

He was a therapeutic distraction—and his anonymity was the best part. She still didn't have a clue who he might be or where he was from.

"Kate?" Caleb said, reminding her she held him hanging in silence. "You still there?"

"Yeah. Sorry." Kate smacked fingertips to her forehead.

"All right. Thought I lost you for a sec. What's up?"

Like she was about to tell him she'd received a fancy card from a human enigma. "Nothing. Let me call you right back."

Kate tugged the paper from the card and laughed out loud at the image of a playful-looking monkey swinging from a tree vine. "Hang in there," the message read, simply signed BB.

A flutter went through Kate. Prior to this, she'd been in a bad mood since talking to Dad while on her break at work. Mom had asked for a court date and Dad actually gave it. Their nonchalance about the whole thing had sickened and upset Kate. Now, standing here, BB's gift eased the emotional strain. "I love monkeys," she whispered. "How'd he know?"

Or maybe he didn't. It could be coincidence and this just happened to be the animal on a message he'd picked out. She didn't care either way. All that mattered was that the card made Kate feel cared for.

This person, whoever he was, had thoughtfulness and stealth that intrigued her. She reminded herself that it could be dangerous to become *too* intrigued. Still, she decided, there'd be no harm in filing the paper memento and its predecessors firmly away, both in her mind, heart and in her keepsake box at home.

She looked around EPTC's parking lot and the woodsy area surrounding it, but her military training had already alerted her that he was long gone. Otherwise she'd have sensed him watching.

She slid into her seat, relishing the relief of taking a load off her aching feet and back. "Long night," she mouthed to the greeting-card monkey grinning up at her from the passenger seat.

She called Caleb back. When he answered she said, "I wondered if you'd want to help me watch Tia for a few hours this evening so Bri and Ian can go out on a real date. A nice one. This is the only night Ian's not on schedule, but I just finished a long shift, and if I watch Tia alone, I might nod off."

"How many hours we talking?" He seemed to be

chewing something. The strawberry Twizzlers he lived on, perhaps? Or maybe gum. Spearmint, like the bandit?

She scowled at her musings. She must be exhausted. That was the only reasonable explanation for the unruly direction of her thoughts. She'd go home, take a nap and head over to Bri's this afternoon with a clear head and heart.

But first, she had to get an answer from Caleb. "Long enough for them to see a movie and have dinner. Well?"

"Wish I could, Kate, but I have plans. Fantastic idea, though."

That couldn't possibly be disappointment singeing her tummy. Could it? "No worries." Kate forced her curiosity down as to what he might be doing on a Friday night. None of her business.

"I'll see you at work, Kate."

Soon as he hung up, Kate wished the call had lasted longer. Weird.

Hours later, a deafening tone assaulted Kate's ears and infringed on her sleep. She smacked at the alarm, confused as to why it was still buzzing before she figured out the culprit was her cell phone. "Do you have a death wish?" she mumbled into the phone.

"Pardon?" Caleb's voice drew her swiftly from her mental fog.

She raked a hand across her hair and stared at the clock. Four. Four in the evening or in the morning? It seemed dark outside, but not quite dark enough to be the middle of the night. "Sorry. I was asleep and I hate getting woke up. What day is it?"

He chuckled. "Still Friday. I'm calling because Mother Nature cancelled my plans for this evening. Still want company watching Tia?"

She smoothed her top and put flip-flops on. "Sure, sounds good."

"What time?"

"Come over to Bri's now, far as I'm concerned. I'll meet you on her side deck and we'll surprise them. I have movie tickets and a dinner voucher to the Golden Terrace for them."

"Ah, GT. I heard they rock the best steaks in the state."

"Yeah. See you at Bri's cabin in a few." Kate wasn't about to suggest she and Caleb go eat there sometime. Golden Terrace was the kind of romantic place a man took a date to.

"I see what you mean about the weather," Kate said when he joined her on Bri's deck. "We're under a severe thunderstorm watch."

"Yep. I have a weather radio and flashlights." He slid his backpack off his shoulders but it caught in his hoodie zipper. "The temp dropped twenty degrees in a matter of hours."

She reached to unhook his backpack strap from his zipper and they both stilled when the back of her hand brushed his chest. Her mouth dried. "Ready?" she managed and stepped back.

The too-careful, quiet way he watched her clued her in he'd noticed. Had he felt that kinetic flash upon contact, too? Hopefully not, or things would just get weird between them. Bad enough that Eagle Point's Cupid Posse seemed intent on throwing them together.

Caleb gestured toward the door. "Ladies first."

She nodded. "Surprise!" Kate announced as they strode in.

"Yay!" Tia squealed and rushed them like a little linebacker. She hugged their legs, squishing them a little too closely together for Kate's peace of mind.

"Ian must've had a heads-up. He's already grinning and dressed up," Caleb observed, laughing. "Bri, you look as shocked as the baby raccoon Mom caught on this very kitchen counter ten years ago." Nostalgia must have hit Caleb hard. He stilled and frowned for a moment, but recovered quickly.

Ian was still grinning at Bri so they didn't notice.

"I've got stuff scattered all over the passenger seat of my car," Ian admitted. "I'll go clean it up so we can head out."

"I'll help." Caleb rushed out the door after Ian, avoiding eye contact with Kate on the way. Man, he was super shy or antisocial or…something. Kate couldn't put her finger on it.

Bri gushed her thanks and went to dress for their dinner date.

Caleb returned only moments later, wearing a scowl. Apparently Ian had declined Caleb's help and sent him back in. Was Ian part of the Cupid Posse, too? No, he couldn't be. Ian knew her so well—he had to know that a die-hard military guy like Caleb was completely wrong for her.

Kate bumped Caleb's shoulder, trying not to be distracted by hard, meticulously sculpted muscles straining taut sleeves. "You okay, soldier? I noticed that raccoon memory sort of threw ya."

His ears reddened. "You have *no* idea." He leaned in, so he could speak out of his sister's earshot. "I can't afford to be homesick. I have to stay focused to make ranger school."

"I heard it's grueling." Kate veered them over to help

Tia, who was about to overfeed a vivid blue fan-tailed Betta fish.

Caleb knelt, peering into the star-shaped bowl. Tia met his gaze over the rim. "Her name is Jonah. She might look small but she can bite your head off in a second if she wants."

Caleb grinned. "Is that right?"

"Yes. She lives in Nineveh." Tia indicated the tank and its décor.

"*She,* huh? Well, Miss Jonah sounds pretty tough, but she's also mighty pretty. In fact, especially with those colors of hers, she reminds me of—" Caleb clamped his mouth shut. Paled. Cast cursory glances at Kate. "N-never mind."

Moments later, Bri emerged from her room, all dressed up. In the rush of hugs and goodbyes as she and Ian headed out for their date, Kate didn't get the chance to ask Caleb why he'd cut himself off like that. But the thought of it still bugged her.

What had he really been about to say? Something not kid-appropriate? That didn't seem like him.

So why was he avoiding her eyes, and what had he done to make him look so guilty?

Chapter Five

Kate. He'd almost said that Miss Jonah reminded him of Kate.

And that would have been fine, if he'd left the similarities at them both being pretty and tough. But no, he'd mentioned the colors.

Miss Jonah's sapphire-and-silver markings reminded him of something he wasn't supposed to have seen—moonlight reflecting off the elaborate, shimmery Mardi Gras–style gown Kate wore that night on the patio. Jonah's sleek shape and willowy blue-black fins resembled the feathers fanning Kate's fancy mask, the one he'd removed to wipe away her tears.

He'd almost voiced the comparison.

He needed to be more careful. Period.

Caleb knelt on a rug woven with zigzag forest creatures next to Tia, who was raptly driving her doll around in a toy boat. Thunder rumbled outside, and the next thing Caleb knew, a frightened Mistletoe dived straight into Caleb's lap.

Caleb nuzzled the dog when the pup trembled. "It's all right, buddy. I won't let that storm get ya."

"Caleb," Kate called from the kitchen where she was

pulling together some dinner for them. She nodded toward Tia who peered up at him with a fearful yet longing expression.

He opened his arms. She scrambled into his lap next to the dog. She trembled just as badly. Caleb wasn't prepared for the powerful emotions sweeping him when Tia snuggled against him and said in a small voice, "Uncle C, I'm scared."

"I'm right here. Kate and I will make sure you're safe."

"But what if there's a tornado?" Tia whimpered.

"We have a basement at the trauma center."

"But not here?" She clutched the edges of her pink tutu. Her fearful tone made him hold her tighter. Protectiveness he'd never known roared up and made him want to fight a tornado with his bare fists if he had to, to protect her. He tucked her closer, resting his chin atop her head. She relaxed against him. No better feeling in the world than knowing he'd graduated in her heart to being *Uncle C*.

How much more awesome would it be to have a child call him Daddy? Caleb quickly rejected the temptation to daydream about it. It would happen someday, but he had other goals that needed to come first. He shored up his mental ranger training plan. Royally spoiling a niece would have to suffice for a few years.

Kate joined them on the rug with a bowl of fruit salad. "We'll keep a close eye on the weather, okay?"

Tia nodded and nestled closer to Caleb when thunder rolled again. This time, though, held securely in his arms, she didn't flinch. It amazed Caleb how trusting Tia was of him. He knew from Bri trust didn't come easy to Tia since her mother abandoned her. He thought of Levi and Asher and all they must be going through. Everyone knew deployment's collateral damage on relationships. He understood Kate's reluctance to date anyone involved in the military, since becoming a civilian.

The dog sniffed the bowl. Kate lifted the food from his reach. "If you wanna wash up, I'll put Mistletoe in his crate for a nap and we can have some of this." She indicated her salad.

Seeing it, he realized why it had taken so long to make. It looked elaborate, like something out of a world-class cooking magazine. He studied Kate's pretty face, pleased they shared a love for creative cooking and baking. Because…because friends should have things in common. And that was exactly what they were.

Once reseated and enjoying the fruit salad Kate distributed, Caleb turned up the TV, set to the local news. The weatherman was on the screen, pointing out red areas on the map. After a while, Kate met his gaze and the most brilliant smile graced her face as her eyes fell on Tia, resting on his chest. Caleb looked down, surprised to see her soundly sleeping.

"What should I do?" He felt out of sorts, kidwise.

"Just hold her. She obviously feels safe with you. Sometimes, girls just need to be held."

Like that night on the patio?

The inclement weather had mostly calmed, but a last, rumbling bit of thunder made Tia frown in her sleep. Kate brushed Tia's forehead and hummed. The maternal gesture turned Caleb into a puddle. To lessen the intimacy of the moment, he whispered, "You're a terrible singer," in low tones. Kate smiled and kept on singing. He liked that about her.

Though she really was a bad singer, he found himself drawn to the words. "Who sings that for real? Like, professionally?"

"Thankfully, not me." She snickered. "Mixed artists. It's contemporary worship." The news switched to a commercial, showing happy dolphins frolicking in blue-green waves. Kate chuckled at the sight. "So apparently Mitch was attacked by a dolphin."

The mental image made Caleb burst out laughing. Tia's head wobbled up. "I'm sorry, sweetness," he whispered to Tia.

Kate's eyebrows flew up.

It took every ounce of self-control he had not to react. Why had he said "sweetness"? Ugh! He was very bad at this double-life, incognito stuff. Maybe he wouldn't make a good ranger after all. But he wasn't bad at it when he was BB, just as himself.

Besides, he needed to do the one thing Dad tried but failed at: becoming an army ranger. How many times before leaving had Dad scoffed that Caleb would never amount to anything? Becoming a ranger was Caleb's only way to disprove the words that had sabotaged his confidence and surety growing up.

Caleb's lack of reaction must have pacified Kate, because she visibly relaxed. "Is 'sweetness' a term of endearment used by all the natives here or something?" She pulled a puzzle box out of the side table.

He laughed. "Yeah, by aborigine yard gnomes crouching in the forest, air-traffic controlling all the flying squirrels Tia says hide in the woods." Bri had told Caleb Tia dragged yard ornaments to the forest edge, creating a make-believe land there.

Kate smirked and smacked his arm. "I'm just curious, since you grew up here, if many people from here say it."

"Pretty much. This is part of the South, and our preference for sweetness has to do with the sugary tea I think." Let her think he was dense.

She cleared her throat. "I have a—friend—who I've heard say that. I'm not sure he lives around here, is all. I'd like to find him. Reconnect."

That could be a problem. "Have you looked for his contact info online?" Caleb offered.

"That's a great suggestion other than I don't know his real—" Kate stopped and scowled. Caleb knew her bristle meant she felt she'd shared too much. "Anyway, it's no big deal." She stood quickly, clearly looking for an escape, and took the chance to turn off the TV and put in a CD, instead. By the time she came back to sit again, her face was calm once more.

They settled into a comfortable kind of quiet and Caleb let the music drift over him. "I like that." He slipped the *Seventh Day Slumber* CD cover from the holder and viewed words to the song, "From the Inside Out." This must be the worship music she'd mentioned earlier. Caleb felt himself softening inside.

"Worship heals us." Kate seemed to sense it touching him. "Especially when we respond to it and sing it back to God."

"I hope you listen to it often, then, and that it helps you."

She winced, then scowled. "*I'm* perfectly fine."

"Sure you are. And my Twizzlers are armed and dangerous."

That didn't go over well, proving once more she was not about to open up to him as Caleb. Not yet. He let it go.

Since Tia's breathing pattern changed, Caleb carried her to the love seat and Kate covered her with a blanket. They returned to the coffee table and started picking out the puzzle's corner and edge pieces. "I love Ron DiCianni paintings," she mused.

He eyed the box then Kate. "Mom did, too. This was hers."

"I'm sorry for your loss, Caleb. And for Bri's."

"Thanks for being here for her. It helped. I'll never regret my service, but I wish I could have found a way to be there for Bri, too."

She nodded. "May I ask why you want to be a ranger?"

He froze. Caleb wasn't at all sure he was ready to talk to Kate about the reasons he wanted—needed—to become a ranger. About his struggles with feelings of worthlessness, his ache to prove himself, his fears that he'd never be good enough.

Maybe it wasn't just Kate who didn't want to open up.

"You can ask."

Wow. He wasn't budging an inch on this one.

"Okay, why do you want to be a ranger?"

"Because I can."

She resisted asking if he'd thought it through. Instead, she prayed that his reasons for pursuing a lifelong military career would be sound, and worth all the worry it would put his family through. Kate could scarcely bear the thought of having to help Bri bury her only brother.

If she were to be honest, life for her would already not be the same without Caleb. And she'd only *really* known him and his quiet strength for a few weeks. How much more loss would Bri feel as his sibling, should the unthinkable happen?

Tia stirred. Kate thought back to the moment when she'd realized that the little girl had fallen asleep in Caleb's arms. She discovered, with growing annoyance, she had to work entirely too hard to stop remembering how handsome Caleb had looked holding the child protectively close. Well, he *was* handsome.

It was just…his holding Tia and comforting the dog in this cozy little amber cabin put him in a warm domestic light. It appealed to Kate in ways that set inner warning flares. It was the situation that drew her, surely, and not the man, right?

She needed to force herself to continue to view him as a friend, perhaps even as a brother by proxy, but never as a romantic prospect. A text bleeped, distracting her from her thoughts.

A loud thunder crash jolted Tia. Startled, she fell off the couch and started crying. Kate could also hear Mistletoe whine from his crate. Kate got the dog.

Caleb gathered Tia. "It's okay, sw—hon."

Resting against him, she rubbed her eyes, dually determined to conk back out and wake herself up. Sleep lost the war. Tia's eyes brightened as she peered adoringly at him. "I'm not a swan, silly. I'm princess of the frilly dolls. Sit." She scrambled down and dragged boxes from the shelf. Kate melted, observing this.

"Oh. Pardon me." Caleb humored Tia, who directed him to an easier, kid-friendly puzzle.

Kate retreated to the kitchen to read her text. Today's medical update from Mom mentioned not one word about Dad. Nor did it address Kate's suggestion of counseling. The text simply, and sadly, stated Grandpa hadn't responded to changes in medication, but Kate didn't need to come. Yet.

Stress clenched Kate's shoulders when she thought of all the trauma-center work she had to accomplish soon. She'd fall seriously behind if she left town to visit Grandpa. Yet she didn't want to regret not going if Grandpa didn't pull through. She had one job and one grandpa, and she could replace her job. Except she'd moved here to help found the trauma center with Mitch and Ian after being deployed with them. EPTC was the result of battlefield dreams. She couldn't bail on them now. Not unless Grandpa's situation grew truly dire. Kate felt torn and troubled.

She eyed the window, knowing it was foolhardy to wish a certain bandit were here to talk to. She shifted gears to study Caleb's profile, suspecting he'd be a willing listener.

Yes, but he might share her struggles with Bri, which would ruin Bri's elation and courtship. Bri needed to enjoy an easy season. Her last was cold, dark, brutal. Caleb's, too, with having lost their mom. No, she couldn't confide in Caleb. Kate glanced at the barren night. No bandit. She was on her own.

She started the dishes and protested when Caleb tried to help. "Enjoy your niece," she said. It wasn't just about wanting to take care of things herself. She also needed more space and time to clear her thoughts than sharing the kitchen with him and his broad chest would allow. She was just having a tough time tonight. That's all. Tomorrow would, hopefully, be better. But it was hard work convincing herself of that.

Especially since the heartening effects of a silly monkey card and it's "Hang in there" message had long worn off.

Maybe she could communicate back with the bandit? Leave notes of her own? While he'd been leaving things in different places, changing it up, probably to keep from getting caught, she did long for one more real conversation with him. Another chance to unload her woes without fear of letting people down. It might be silly, but BB felt like a lifeline right now.

Kate couldn't talk to Bri, or to Caleb because of Bri—and because of their other circumstances. Ian and

Mitch's assignment of his training under her supervision sealed her inability to show weakness around him. That he was now her charge and coworker meant she had to stay strong in his eyes.

Never let them see you sweat.

Her war-decorated dad and staunch, tenacious nursing-instructor mother, a stickler for perfection, had taught her as much. Yet, as Kate pondered their precarious lives now, for the first time since growing up, she began to question all she had known and become because of their adroit gifts and guidance.

Or misguidance?

Was it not actually a good thing to be ultra-capable in the eyes of others and unable to show weakness?

Unwilling to mentally dishonor her parents or their loving efforts, Kate shook the questions off for now and returned to the living room to an adorable scene. Tia and Caleb huddled like close buddies over a colorful, near-complete puzzle.

"Miss Kate? Let's have a tea party," Tia announced.

Caleb chuckled and slouched. "You two have fun with that."

Tia scowled and propped tiny fists on her hips. She marched up and planted herself in front of him.

He looked up with slowly arching brows. "May I help you?"

"Yes. You most uncertainty may."

To Caleb's credit, he bit his lip to stop himself from correcting Tia's word usage. He did grin, though, and it shouldn't nearly be as delicious to Kate. Tia was known for using mile-long words, but often the complete wrong word for the context.

"I want. To have. A tea party," Tia said firmly and

tugged Caleb toward the coffee table. "And you. Will be. A princess."

Kate's mouth twitched as Caleb slogged, doomed and wide-eyed, but without protest, to the table. He looked unable to say no to Tia in all her convincing cuteness and glory. The guy deserved the Uncle of the Year award. Mistletoe slinked under the table. His mouth fell into a pant that made him appear to be laughing at Caleb's uncomfortable but funny predicament.

"Sure, leave me behind and go hide," Caleb teased the pup.

Tia gasped. "Oh, no! I forgot! I don't have a tea set!"

Rather than shout praises, Caleb plopped down next to the coffee table, looking very much in problem-solving mode. "No sweat. We'll make some tea stuff." He grabbed construction paper from a box near the table then glue, tape and scissors. Tia, and admittedly Kate, watched in wonder as Caleb drew a mirror shape of a teapot on poster board then cut it out.

"This is what it'll look like." He folded it to have a base and set it upright. "You need to give it some color."

"Ooh, cool! Yay!" Tia shoved the construction paper aside and popped open a tub of bright beads, reflective sequins and glittery markers.

Caleb laughed. "Bling works, too." It wasn't until he caught Kate's gaze that she realized she was ardently staring. "I could use an assistant teacup maker over here. You game?" he asked.

She smiled and the trio fashioned a quite elaborate and impressive tea set out of cardstock and craft supplies.

Afterward, Tia gathered her dolls and stuffed animals and placed them in itty chairs Caleb had brought to the "tea table."

"Miss Kate, you didn't invite any of yours." Tia sounded sincerely concerned. "We can't leave them out!"

"I don't have any stuffed animals. Never have."

"Never *ever?*" Tia sucked in a disbelieving breath.

"Nope. My parents never thought I needed one, I guess."

Tia stared openmouthed. "That's crazy! Who doesn't need a soft bunny or a teddy bear to hug?" She sighed, clearly channeling her father. "I will have to have a word with your parents."

That made Kate laugh, initially. But then a slice of dark pain went through her when she thought of all the fond memories of childhood with the trio of herself, Mom and Dad. Despite the lack of stuffed animals, she'd thought they were all so happy together. The devastating possibility of her parents not reconciling hit her again. Unlike Caleb and Bri, she was an only child and didn't have siblings to lean on. If her parents split, that was it. Thoughts of ending up alone in the world welled irrational panic in Kate.

Caleb must have noticed her struggle because he scooted closer than Kate felt comfortable with, being this emotionally fragile. She stiffened her spine and tried to prepare what she would say if he asked her if she was okay. He didn't. Instead, he sat near and interacted with Tia who, thankfully, didn't pick up on Kate's being on the verge of tears.

Don't break down, Dalton.

Caleb kept the conversation with Tia lively. He kept the dialogue between the two of them, as if he sensed speech in any form would be iffy for Kate right now. Speech without bursting into tears that is. She appreciated his perceptiveness, yet hoped he wouldn't be offended she couldn't open up to him.

"Tia, I'm surprised you don't have a real tea set," Caleb remarked when the paper teapot fell over for the fifth time.

"I did, but I gave it to a little girl whose toys burned up in a fire."

Caleb hunkered. "My goodness, how sad. That was sweet of you to give your toys to her, though. That was really thoughtful and kind."

"I even gave her Blink, my favorite doll." Tia's lips warbled. Kate's heart clenched, thinking of the fire victims.

"I bet Blink's her favorite toy now, and one she'll love and take care of forever." Caleb's voice softened like sweet taffy.

"The little girl's mommy got dead in the fire, too. Doctor Lockhart cried and cried." Tia clicked her tongue. Kate hated that Tia had been at the trauma center when the victims came in. But Bri had been out of town and Ian hadn't had time to take Tia anywhere before EMTs brought the victims.

Caleb looked horrified but kept his voice calm and soothing. "I'm sure a lot of people cried."

Kate sent Tia to get Mistletoe fresh water, food and a doggy treat then asked Caleb, "Have you met her yet?"

"Doctor Lockhart? I don't think so, why?"

"Just wondered." Kate nibbled her lips. Then leaned in. "Her name's Clara, just so you know. I'm worried about her. She took an emergency leave of absence after the fire victims came in. She hasn't been back to work." Kate watched Tia carefully and kept her voice low. "She's pretty secretive about her life, but I think Clara may have lost a child in a fire because she seemed *really* traumatized."

"That's rough. She won't talk about it, though?"

Kate shook her head. "Can't say I blame her."

"You don't have to be strong all the time, Kate."

She stared sternly at him. "That's a matter of opinion. It's also not up for discussion. Besides, this isn't about me."

He nodded slowly. "Fair enough. For now."

Kate's straight white teeth clenched, but Caleb didn't let it daunt him. He was determined to get her to a point where she would open up to people in her life, starting with him. He had three months left to make that happen.

Problem was, BB could hinder that. Caleb wanted to laugh at the irony of competing with himself.

His humor faded when news of a house fire scrolled across his phone's EMT scanner app. He thought about Dr. Clara Lockhart, the young anesthesiologist Kate mentioned.

Tia came back from tending to Mistletoe and flanked her hands on Kate's face. "Dr. Lockhart's pretty and you are, too. You look like that most bee-you-tea-ful princess on TV."

Kate's eyebrows arched. "Oh, really? Which one?"

Tia climbed Kate's lap. "The real one who married the prince who flies the planes. You're even named after her."

Caleb reclined against the couch skirt. "Kate Middleton, the duchess. And Tia's right. You're a dead ringer for her."

Kate's eyebrows pinched as she set the princess doll down. "Hmm. I'll have to study her out. I don't watch TV much."

"How come?" Tia scooted between Kate and Caleb.

"The war news bothers me because my father is serving overseas. Plus, I don't want to be tempted to start missing the action, my military unit comrades or my old life."

Tia leaned in sweetly, nose to nose. "Do you sometimes?"

"I do." Kate bumped foreheads gently with Tia.

"Even though my mom was mean, I sometimes miss her, too. She was my old life." Tia scrambled to her feet and sped to Miss Jonah's tank. "You could watch Miss Jonah with me. A fish tank isn't like anybody's old life."

Kate laughed and Caleb smiled in the midst of his ringtone. "Excuse me, I need to take this." Caleb went on the side deck to answer Asher's call. "Hey, man. How ya doin'?"

"Eh, you know. Hangin' in, I guess. You?"

"I'm good, man. You and Levi have been on my mind."

"We're makin' it. Things'll get better."

"Yeah, they will." Caleb thought of Ian and Tia and how life had turned around for them the past few months.

"So, I wanted to check in and ask—how's the physical training coming along?"

"Real good. I get up at 4:00 a.m. to run and do the rigorous outdoor stuff before it gets hot. The PJs gave me keys to their Refuge Drop Zone gym. I hit the weights, then swim. I spend no less than four hours a day working out. I hope it's enough."

"It will be, Landis. You have what it takes. How's Kate?"

Caleb looked at her through the window. "Good. We've gotten to spend more time as friends since I've been here. Bri's glad."

"I'm sure. She probably hopes it'll turn into more."

"Not gonna happen. Our lives are going in opposite

directions." Caleb couldn't deny feeling regret at that. Strange. When did that start? It needed to stop.

"Well, I just wanted to see how you're doing. Levi's ready for lunch and begging for pasta. I'd better go figure out how to fix it." Asher chuckled on the other line.

"I'll let you go. Stay cool, man."

"I'm trying, Landis. God's got me, but it's hard."

"Don't lose your faith." That would be a tragedy. "I wish you lived closer. We'd hang and I'd go to church with you."

Asher laughed. "Seriously? If you're not blowing smoke, don't be surprised if we show up on your doorstep someday."

"Hey, if you're looking to relocate, Eagle Point's the place to be. There's Refuge, next town over, too. Place does its best to live up to its name. Keep that in mind, all right?"

"I will. You keep in mind I'm holding you to the whole church thing if me and Levi end up there. 'Bye, now."

Caleb ended the call smiling yet sifting through ambivalent emotion. He needed to work things out with God. He knew he did. He just wasn't sure he was ready. Letting God in meant letting all the anger out. And that would require him to stop hating his dad.

He didn't hate the man himself, really. But he did hate the hurt Dad had caused, and other consequences that Dad's bad choices rained on his, Mom's and Bri's lives.

It fueled his driving need to triumph over his dad, and prove wrong everything the man had said about him. It wasn't a very Christian impulse.

Caleb came back in and sat down on the rug next to Kate. She looked to be about to ask him if everything was okay when Caleb changed the subject.

"Tia, why did you name a girl fish Jonah?"

Tia huffed as delicately as a fairy princess could. "I *didn't.* I named a *boy* fish Jonah but my *dad* didn't apparently know the *difference* between boys and girls yet then. He does now. Little girls will break your eardrums and little boys will break your furniture. That's what Daddy says is the difference. And my daddy is *allllways* right."

"He's most certainly usually right," Kate said, giggling.

Bri and Ian took that prime moment to walk in from their date.

Despite the smattering of uncomfortable moments, Caleb was sorry to see his babysitting gig with Kate come to an end. It had felt far too natural to laugh and talk with her, playing tea party and taking care of Tia. It had all been so warmly, sweetly…domestic.

And that, as much as anything, was why he needed to go home. He'd get some sleep and wake up for his training, and remind himself that domestic was the last thing he needed.

Chapter Six

"See? I was right. You're like a sidewalk shadow a shoe can't detach from," Kate teased. Caleb grinned in reply as he unfolded his tall, bulky frame from Bri's car. They'd arrived separately, but had the same destination—Lem's barbecue welcoming Refuge's PJs back from a pilot rescue mission.

It had been a week since their babysitting adventure, but she'd seen plenty of him since then. Comrades and coworkers had begun to call him her shadow. Not only did they work together remodeling Bri's bunkhouses, but he also was required to follow her around work at EPTC.

"Hello to you, too, Kate."

"No! I want Uncle C to," Tia said as Ian bent to unbuckle her. Ian stepped back with a smile and nodded at Caleb.

Caleb helped Tia out of her booster seat. Or tried. "Okay, someone tell me how this thing works."

Ian had taken the kidless moment of opportunity to drag his fiancée to the cozy gazebo in a private corner of the yard. Kate smiled at the image of the strong, manly soldier struggling to figure out the buckles and straps.

"Move over, Landis." Kate leaned in to help. "It can't

be too hard." Well. Maybe. Bri and Ian must have graduated Tia to a new seat. This one looked as if it required
an engineering degree to operate. She swooshed hair
from her eyes and elbowed Caleb. "It would help if you'd
scoot over and give the expert some room." Plus, his
nearness was messing with her concentration.

He laughed. And stayed right where he was. Gentle
elbow jabs and genteel verbal sparring ensued that boiled
down to two headstrong leaders not used to having to
follow. And both being dead-dog determined to *not* be
the one unable to figure out what should be a simple
buckle release. After moments of Caleb and Kate's con-
joined yet competing attempts, Tia giggled then reached
down and aptly unsnapped the contraption.

"That works, too." Caleb chuckled and lifted Tia out.

"Figures. Ask a kid for help when maneuvering medicine bottles, smartphones, computer technology and for
sure, fortress-caliber car seats." Kate ruffled Tia's hair.
"You really enjoyed watching us sweat that one out,
didn't ya kiddo?"

Tia covered her mouth but the giggle wouldn't be
capped.

Caleb peered past Kate then nodded to Tia. "Hey,
hold this pretty princess for a bit, will ya? I need to talk
to someone."

Kate took Tia and pivoted around to see where Caleb
went.

Her heart sank to her toes. Brock, a PJ, picked Caleb
up on a four-wheeler. They disappeared over the knoll
where Lem had a weight bench in his barn. Probably the
PJ was going to help Caleb train for ranger school. Oh,
well. None of her business.

"Ready for a horsey ride?" Kate galloped with Tia,

whose laughter and squeals permeated the cornfield-flanked yard.

Kate refused to look back or acknowledge the little hope inside that Caleb would rejoin their antics.

"Tia, Lem's getting Bess out!" Bri and Ian announced upon approaching. Kate knew Bess was Lem's faithful tractor.

"Yippee!" Tia launched herself into her dad's arms.

"Where's Caleb?" Bri looked around. Kate bit her lip.

"With Brock." Ian studied Kate shrewdly. Who knew what for?

Bri's forehead furrowed. "Oh." She looked at Kate, as if she wanted to ask her why. But how would Kate know? Caleb was required to follow her around at EPTC. He had no reason to stick close to her the rest of the time.

Ian pointed toward Lem's house. "Bess is ready."

"You okay, Kate?" Bri asked when Ian took Tia.

"It's none of my business who he's with or why, Bri. I hope you don't think I'm interested in your brother. And he's certainly not interested in me." Obviously! Ugh. Who cared?

Bri just stared at Kate silently.

Uh-oh. "Bri? He's *not* interested in me, right?"

"Right. I mean, the only thing on his mind is getting into ranger school."

"No need to worry over me feeling neglected. Caleb and I are enjoying a nice friendship. I don't expect to be his only friend."

Yet Kate couldn't deny the irritability gnawing her when he didn't hang with her for the next two hours.

Eventually Caleb jogged up with a wince on his face. "Hey, sis. Would you be too terribly offended if I jet?"

"You mean leave? With Brock?"

"Yeah. It's important. Otherwise, I'd stay."

Bri shrugged. "Suit yourself. I'll see you at home later?"

"You bet. Thanks for letting me take over your couch so we can renovate cabin seven." He grinned then gave Kate an awkward, hasty wave before sprinting to Brock who tossed Caleb his keys.

All Kate could think as the truck peeled out of Lem's driveway was that he'd never been in that much of a hurry to leave with her.

"They're probably going to train for Caleb's ranger test."

Kate forced neutrality onto her face so Bri wouldn't suspect Kate's discomfort with the idea. Yes, she knew that becoming a ranger was important to Caleb, but she couldn't pretend to be pleased that he'd be taking a position that would put him in so much danger.

Kate's phone bleeped a text from Mom and she immediately knew her day was destined to keep heading downhill.

Honey, you should think about heading to Chicago before long.

She felt Bri radiating concern beside her. She forced herself not to react physically. Instead, Kate called her mom. "How long is 'before long,' Mom?"

"They've given him four months, at best."

Kate swallowed. "At worst?"

A heavy pause. "Weeks. He's gone into a coma, so I...I don't think it'll be long now. I'm sorry, honey. I wish I had better news."

"And Dad?"

"Is at his hotel. He was feeling ill and didn't want to expose your grandfather. Kate, the doc's back. I should go."

Kate hated the deadness on the line, both before and

after Mom actually hung up. Her voice hadn't so much as cracked when discussing Dad. And if they were staying at different hotels, that wasn't a good sign. *Daddy, Mama, please try.*

Kate fought an overwhelming urge to cry. She swallowed the emotion before looking up. She pasted a smile on, but Bri didn't look one bit fooled.

"What's going on?"

"I may need to head to Chicago next month. I should look in on my grandfather. Plus, I'd like to see my dad. He flew in a couple days ago. I forgot to tell you." She hadn't gone to see him yet because she'd wanted to give him and Mom alone time, maybe to reconcile.

Clearly, that wasn't happening. "I think I'll go for a walk. See Lem's rabbits at the hutches on the edge of his land."

"Okay, but are you sure you don't need me?"

"I'm fine. Really. Go find that handsome fiancé of yours. You need time together, and Lem and the PJs are going to keep Tia entertained. When you're ready to leave, you'll have to drag her away from Bess, farm animals and flower beds." Kate smiled at Lem's charming home, literally a houseboat on dry land, which drove his granddaughter Lauren bananas. That was Lem for you. His quirky humor shone through in all the details of his home, including the scarecrows he had lining the fence and gracing the porch swings of his houseboat.

When she walked away, her smile faded, and the full weight of her mother's news hit Kate once she was out for a walk. In a remote field, she let herself break. Raw emotion seeped out, causing rabbits to skitter to cage corners. Kate stayed like that for what might have been an hour, crying in the dusk, then the stars and the moonlight, and wishing…

Foolish! Your bandit is nowhere around.

Kate dug her fingers into the wood and let it scrape her hands like the pain inside scraped at her heart. Tears welled again. This time, they fell silently.

A hand covered her shoulder. She shrieked and whirled.

"Caleb! You scared me to death." Ugh! "You're lucky I didn't attack you." She dashed away tears and scrambled for an excuse to explain them away. How had she not heard him approach?

"I've been here awhile, Kate. Besides, Bri told me about the text and I came back."

"Pity."

"I don't pity you."

"That's not what I meant. I meant it's a pity you had to leave a workout to find me for no reason. I'm fine. I don't need anyone doting over me or expending worry when it's completely unnecessary."

His jaw hardened. "You're more stubborn than I realized."

"Yeah? Well, you and all this unwelcome concern are maddening. Go, Caleb. Spend time with your sister while you can. She misses you." Kate started off.

"Kate, wait." He put his hand on her shoulder again, and it reminded her of her bandit that night on the patio.

"Caleb Frustration Landis, you're making me lose my temper. Let go of me, now." She jerked away, because if she didn't, she'd cave to the compassion in his eyes. Reminded her so much of— No. Stop thinking about *him.* You can't take the bandit so seriously.

BB was nothing more than a distraction. While his notes were nice, they were just a Band-Aid. Her life and her family could not be fixed. Not by anyone.

"I'm here if you need me."

"I don't *need* anyone."

"Incorrect. You might not want to need us, but you do."

His statement cut through her like a scalpel, simply because it was true. And that was the part she hated most of all.

"Go home, Landis. That's an order."

"We're not at work, Kate. You can't boss me around."

"Watch me."

A muscle clicked in his jaw. "Don't shut me out."

"If you won't leave, I will." She pushed past him.

His arm sprang out to stop her. When she tried to go around it, he pulled her in, wrapping his arm around her. Her back rested snugly against his chest and his chin braced the top of her head. "Kate, listen a minute. I can—"

"No, you can't. You can't do anything to help me. You can't fix it. Now let me go!"

With equal reluctance and frustration, he did. She stared him down. "Don't ever do that again."

His nostrils flared and he marched off, leaving her confused and upset. She had wanted him to leave her alone, so why did she ache to rush back into his arms and stay there forever? Or at least until she could suture her emotions back together?

She didn't need this, this growing dependency on people.

Especially not him. He'd be leaving sooner than she wanted to think about. Kate stared at the cornfield edges and just started running. She ran until her legs wanted to fall off. She ran until she could no longer feel her feet or the blisters there. She ran until she had no more tears to cry.

Grandpa was in a coma. And she hadn't gone to see

him in time. She'd lost her chance to say goodbye. She couldn't tell Caleb, or anyone. If she talked, she'd break down. From that point onward, even if she got stronger again later, the people around her would always look back and remember her cracking under pressure.

She couldn't.

She could not be that person in other people's eyes. She had to be strong. Hadn't Grandpa always told her so? To pick herself up by the bootstraps and face life head-on, headstrong?

"Grandpa, I'm trying. I really am. I've failed you in so many ways." Tears tried to force their way out again. Kate choked them back, though no one would see now except scarecrows. She half wished one of them would step out and morph into a bandit.

Stop. Not even he can fix this.

By the time she joined the rest of the party, she'd calmed enough to say faux upbeat goodbyes to Bri and the crew. She thanked Lem for his hospitality and marched toward her Jeep, aware of gunmetal eyes boring into her back. She didn't have to look to know who it was. Her Academy Award–caliber exit might have fooled everyone else, but Caleb had seen her rabbit-hutch tears and knew better.

She fought anger at herself for letting her guard down in public. She'd have to rectify that. Show him at work and elsewhere how strong she really was. Not some crybaby who talked to scarecrows and clung to rabbit cages and sobbed her soul out beneath the stars.

When she reached her car, her heart leaped at the sight of a slip of paper tucked against the windshield. Was it…could it be…had her bandit come through for her just when she needed him the most?

Scolding herself for her trembling hands, she pulled out the paper and unfolded it.

Meet me tonight at midnight, on the seventh lake dock. Hold on, sweetness. We'll get you through this.
BB

That night, Caleb donned the bandit costume with mixed emotions. He knew Kate needed this—needed someone she could talk to without worrying about being strong. He'd tried to be that person for her earlier, but she wouldn't let him. She'd let the bandit, though…so that was who he needed to be.

He walked quietly to the dock, making sure to get there thirty minutes early in case Kate got the bright idea to show early and see from where he came. He'd chosen the seventh lake dock deliberately. He knew that it had a pillar he could hide behind and still talk to her. It was also the darkest dock on the lake at night.

Kate arrived exactly at midnight. Caleb stepped out from the shadows, but not too far.

She stopped. Gasped. "You really came." She drew a slow breath. "I—I'm actually a little surprised you're here. I'm glad, though. How…how did you know I needed you?"

"It doesn't matter," Caleb said, his voice a soft whisper to make it harder to identify. "All that matters is that you needed me, and I'm here. Tell me what's wrong."

He could see her struggling with what she was willing to say. It made him ache to pull her into his arms and hold her until she felt confident and sure of herself again. But no, he'd have to let her take this at her own pace.

"My grandpa…did I tell you about my grandpa last time?"

Caleb shook his head. "How about you tell me now?" He kept his voice carefully low and disguised.

"Grandpa is…" Kate's smile was so sad. "Grandpa's amazing. Tough as nails. Career military. One of the best commanders I've ever seen. But such a good family man, too. When he retired, he was always there for me and my parents. Dad was deployed a lot, and Mom would teach nursing during the day and then practice nursing at night. Grandma and Grandpa were the ones I could count on to always be there for me. To tuck me into bed at night, and read me a story, and help me fall back to sleep when I had a bad dream." She turned to face him and he saw the tears streaming down her face, shining in the moonlight.

This time, he didn't hold himself back. He moved forward and drew her into his embrace. She went willingly. He was so glad he could hold her through this— and yet he had to bite his tongue to keep from scolding her. Why would she only let a stranger hold her like this? If she could accept this comfort from the bandit, then why couldn't she accept it from Caleb?

Great, now I'm thinking of myself in third person. I'm losing it.

"He's been sick for a while now," Kate continued. "But recently, it's gotten worse. Mom's there to take care of him. She said I didn't need to come out, not yet. So I didn't. I told myself it was because I had responsibilities here, and because Mom had everything taken care of. But I think…"

And here it came, Caleb could tell. Here was the part where she'd tell the bandit something she'd never tell anyone else. *Why does she trust him—I mean me—I mean the bandit this much, anyway?*

"I think I just wanted to avoid it all. Avoid seeing Grandpa so sick. Avoid seeing my parents when their marriage is falling apart. Maybe I thought that if I didn't have to watch, if I kept my distance, then I could get used to Grandpa not being in my life and my parents not being in love."

Caleb's hold on her tightened. With a tact he could never quite manage when he was in his own persona, he just knew that this wasn't a time to try to come up with words of comfort or consolation. He didn't even try to wipe her tears away. He just held her and let her cry. After she'd cried herself out, he was rewarded with a tremulous smile.

"Thanks," she said shakily. "That was just what I needed."

Now he wiped away the tears, not with a handkerchief but with his thumb brushing gently against her cheek. "Life is not for the faint of heart, sweetness," he whispered. "It'll hurt you in so many ways."

"I can take it. I just need to learn to be stronger. Tougher." Even as she said the words, her shoulders went back and her spine straightened. She was doing it again—trying to be brave Kate, reliable Kate, always-in-control Kate rather than just letting herself *be*.

"Would you really want that?" he asked as gently as he could. "If you could turn off your emotions and not be bothered by sadness or loss, would you do it? You wouldn't hurt anymore, but you'd miss out on feeling the love and the hope, too."

He half expected her to get angry with him, but instead she just nodded and looked thoughtful.

"You're right," she said at last, so caught up in her

thoughts that she didn't seem to notice the way he nearly staggered at her words. She admitted that he was right? That would never happen if he were outside of his bandit persona. Was it wrong to feel jealous of yourself?

"I've been forgetting to hold on to hope. In fact, I've been grieving for my grandfather's life and my parents' marriage when neither one is over yet."

This time, her smile was so dazzling that it froze him in place. He was barely even aware of her leaning forward and brushing her lips—gently, softly, sweetly—against his. By the time he came back to himself, the kiss was over.

"Thank you," she said. "Truly. You can't imagine how much you've done for me these past few weeks."

And you can't imagine how much you mean to me, Caleb thought to himself. Even though he knew a relationship between them could never be possible, Kate had come to be so incredibly important to him. If this ridiculous charade with the costume was what it took to help her hold herself together, then that was what he'd do. No matter how badly it stung that she'd lean on the bandit but not on Caleb, as himself.

"So what will you do now?" he asked.

"Go visit my grandpa as soon as I can get away."

Caleb nodded. "Good idea. And maybe you could take someone with you, to help you deal with everything, so you don't have to take care of it all alone." *Maybe someone a little over six feet tall with dark hair and gray eyes, answering to the name Caleb...*

But Kate was already shaking her head. "No, I don't think so. I can handle it. Thanks to you."

She left then, and Caleb tried to take comfort in the way her step seemed lighter, less weary. He'd helped. But had it been enough? Could it ever be enough? Could some anonymous stranger in a mask ever truly be there for Kate in the way she needed?

No. But Caleb could. And he promised himself right then and there that he *would.* Whether Kate liked it or not.

"Pink?"

Kate squared her feet but smiled at Caleb. "Pink *camouflage.*"

A pink camouflage tape measure. It shouldn't fit, but somehow it did. It was perfectly Kate.

She was in her element the next day as they knelt over saws, paint and plywood at Eagle Point Church's basement, building props for Lem's storybook ball.

He chuckled and slid a piece of plywood in front of his knees, intending to hand-draw a king's scepter on it, then cut it out.

She scooted it her way and chalked a queen's throne scroll instead.

"I see how this is gonna go."

"What?" She blinked those long lashes far too innocently.

"Yeah. You're not gettin' my power tools."

"I wouldn't dream of it." Yet she practically drooled over the Dremel tool assortment rattling as he opened its box.

"Right." He laughed and arranged his tools in an arc.

She rearranged them, in Kate OCD fashion. "What's the plan?"

"I'm spontaneous. I don't need a plan. Furthermore, you don't like to take orders, and I'm a born leader. So go work over there." He pointed to the far corner of the room.

"No, actually. This way, *my way,* is more interesting."

He laughed, unable to be aggravated. "*Your way* could lead to bloodshed." He scooted four feet away from Kate, grabbed a fresh piece of plywood and placed a castle turret pattern on it.

The previous night, pushing his way into her life and her problems had seemed like such a good idea. But in the clear light of day, he'd started to question himself. Did he have any right to get involved in her personal life when he wasn't planning to stay? Would that be fair to her? Would it be fair to him? He had his own goals, his own dreams. He should be focusing on those rather than entrenching himself in someone else's life.

But his plan to place some more distance between them was dying a rapid death, thanks to Kate's stubbornness. She'd landed in his personal space like a jet swooping on a target. "Make up your mind, Landis. Are we cutting or drawing?"

"We? I was doing both fine before you got here," he teased.

"You like to work alone or what?" Her eyes practically went cross-eyed at the notion. Pretty eyes.

He looked away. "Sometimes alone works better for me."

Wood clattered. "Well, it doesn't for me." She abandoned her project to help trace his. Obviously, Kate was used to not only working with a team but being in full charge of that team.

Caleb switched gears to sand rough edges off wood patterns he'd cut hours before she got here.

She unplugged his electric sander and shoved sandpaper pieces at him. "The intricate patterns need to be done by hand."

Caleb sat back on his haunches. "Have fun with that, then."

"So that's what you do? The going gets rough…and you quit?" Yes, he did exactly that. Walked away from God when life got tough. Kate was spot-on. Not that he was ready to admit it yet.

He popped the tab on a soda and used it to hide his expression. "I'm not quitting. I'm resting, while I watch you sand all that by hand."

"Ha! Like you're going to get out of helping me. Besides, God Himself says it's not good for man to be alone."

He snorted, and Kate frowned. "What's your hang-up with God anyway, Landis?"

He resisted the urge to go back to arguing about the sanding. He knew Kate wouldn't let this go though, so he might as well spit it out now. "I asked God to provide for Mom when Dad abandoned us, yet He let her lose the court battle over alimony. When I deployed, I asked him to watch over my family. He took Mom. I asked him to help save our lodge from foreclosure, and it ended up catching fire, causing Bri more stress, time, money and pressure from the bank."

She sat silent at first then said, "I'm glad God had Mitch, Ian, Lauren and me here to watch over Bri through it all. And I'm sorry your dad left."

"His choice."

"His loss."

"Sorry you're going through stuff with your parents, Kate."

She stiffened as if hit with a small-caliber bullet. "Life goes on." Rising to her feet, she turned her back to him and occupied herself sanding wood that would be a scepter by Sunday.

When the going got rough…

It struck him as odd that the same renowned hero

known for being so brave on battlefields was so steely set on staying safe in a civilian setting. She'd put her life on the line…but not her heart.

Caleb didn't like the disappointment he felt that she still wasn't willing to open up to him, especially after the way she'd confided in the bandit the previous night.

Caleb reminded himself of his decision not to get too involved. Getting her to open up to *him* as she had the bandit would take time he wasn't sure he'd be allotted. Especially since his C.O. had called this morning to warn him things were heating up.

"Things often get worse before they get better," he said from the floor where he knelt now, ready to saw the shape of a castle drawbridge out of the wood she'd sanded.

"Kind of like the night is darkest just before the dawn." A wistfulness in her voice and the stilling of her shoulders as she spoke let him know his words—as the bandit—were giving her the strength she needed to get through.

Caleb fell into his own silence as he fired up the saw and went to work on the wood. Strangely, despite his and Kate's vastly opposite working methods, they meshed productively.

At one point he raised his face to find Kate standing directly beneath an enormous wall cross. The vibrant symbol hung there like a sentinel watching over them, as if it could see. He felt odd, sitting calmly inside a church when he was still so angry with God.

Yet he equally knew that an incalculable amount of mercy resided there that would keep the walls from caving in on him. If God had this much mercy on Caleb, who was openly crabby and actively avoiding God, how much more profound the mercy would be that He'd lavish on Kate, still running hard after God, despite all the loss she faced.

Half doubtful and half hopeful, Caleb sent a prayer up above.

If it's true you heal, Kate's heart could use a touch.

Chapter Seven

"I need an awkward favor," Bri admitted as she helped Kate cut decorative storybook ball costume material.

Kate stretched a piece of purple silk out. "Sure. Shoot."

"Ian and I want to go to an engaged couples' retreat hosted by our church this weekend in St. Louis from Friday to Monday."

"Need someone to watch Tia?"

"Yeah. I was thinking you and Caleb could handle it, since you're both off and not on call. He's already agreed to it. I promise I'm not matchmaking. I'd mentioned to Caleb I was going to ask you and he offered to help out, too, if you wouldn't mind him being here. He's really getting attached to Tia and wants to spend as much time with her as he can."

From Bri's anxious expression Kate realized that she felt guilty asking for help with Tia. Allowing Caleb to share the babysitting load would ease Bri's guilt and let her fully unplug and enjoy her weekend with Ian. Plus, she seemed sincere about not matchmaking. "I'd love to help out. You guys need to get away."

"Sure you're okay with watching Tia three overnights?"

"Friday through Monday? I'm fine with it and I'm sure Caleb is, too. Tia'd enjoy both of us here, anyway. I'll crash on your couch."

"Caleb already made up his mind to give you his room."

"Really? That was sweet of him."

"Thanks for doing this, Kate. I'll return the favor when you have kids." Bri tugged red suede from the fabric bin.

"I'd like a husband first," Kate said impishly.

"Yeah, like you have time to date. What about the bandit?"

"Right. I need someone stable. Not someone only meant to be a bright spot for a season."

Bri nibbled her lip, which made Kate wonder what she was hiding. Or had Kate's comment about the bandit only being around for a season reminded Bri that Caleb would be leaving soon, too?

"Bri, why is it so important to Caleb to be a ranger?"

Bri gave Kate a pensive glance. "That's his story to tell. But I will say it has a lot to do with his need to prove himself to our father. He really did a number on my brother. Yet Caleb was, even at ten years of age, a more responsible man than my dad ever thought about being."

"Parents' words are powerful. Kids are impressionable and sometimes grow into the words adults speak over them." Kate considered Caleb. Whose acts and words had fashioned his identity? His mom's? Dad's? A teacher perhaps?

Someone did a lot of good because he was a phenomenal guy.

Kate sighed. "I hope when I'm a parent I don't make the wrong kind of difference. I'm so sorry you two had to endure that." Hurt swirled inside Kate for Bri, but more so for Caleb, the unsettled sibling. "I hope he's making the best decision."

"Ranger school? He's not confident he has what it takes."

Kate shifted. She almost wished she agreed. He'd be safer that way. "I am. He totally has what it takes."

"That scares me. I don't want something to happen to him. Militia often target special operatives. I'd be lost without him. And you're becoming good friends… so would you, right?"

Kate hug-braced Bri's shoulders. "You know the old adage—worry is as pointless as paying interest on debts you don't owe. Put him in God's hands, Bri, and leave him there. Okay?"

Bri nodded. "I'm trying." She unfolded a bolt of pink taffeta.

"And you're right. I'd be lost without him, too. Who else would I have left to royally annoy without having to worry about getting my head bitten off?"

That made Bri laugh. "True. Caleb is so laid back, he's horizontal. I miss him so much when he's overseas, but at least God sent you, Kate. You're like the sister I never had but always wanted."

For some reason Bri's words flared images of what being a sister-in-law to her could be like. Kate scowled at her rebellious imagination, because the only way to become Bri's sister-in-law would be to marry her brother. Not happening.

His heart was too fond of camouflage for her comfort.

"Uncle C!" Tia didn't even let Caleb get all the way through the door before she threw herself at his knees. Caleb patted her back, looking up to grin at Kate who stood off to the side. After the hug, Tia dashed back to her bedroom to play. So much for her excitement over the arrival of her second babysitter for the weekend.

"Sorry I'm a little late." He presented Kate with a sheepish grin and a speeding ticket. "I drove Brock's sports car here. I'm not used to the level of power with so little pedal effort. You ready? I want to take you and Tia to dinner."

"Oh? I was going to throw some BLTs together."

"Nah. Save your energy. Let's eat in style."

Kate frowned. "Like, where?"

"The Golden Terrace."

"What? We can't go there. I'm not dressed for it. Besides that, they require reservations on weekends. Not to mention I'm pinching my dimes, remember?"

There had to be more to it than that. Kate looked on the verge of panic, and she didn't spook easily. But he wasn't going to be dissuaded. What was wrong with wanting to take a lovely lady and his favorite niece out for a nice meal?

"It's my treat. I made reservations and you can wear something of Bri's. She has dressy duds in her humongous closet. Plus, Tia likes to dress up. Which reminds me... Be right back." He dashed to the car and returned with store packages.

Tia emerged from the bedroom pulling a wagon full of dolls. "We're havin' us a slumber party. Even you, Uncle C."

Caleb knelt, picking up a doll. "So, who do we have here?"

"That is Sing." Tia pulled a string in the doll's back and a melody flowed from a tiny speaker. Tia plucked another doll up. "This is Giggles." Tia pushed a foot button. The doll wiggled and, well, giggled.

Caleb picked up another. "What's this one's name?"

"Dance." Tia showed its ballerina twirling capabilities then lifted another doll. "She's Shine." The doll lit all over.

"I see a common theme. You name dolls after what they do."

"Or maybe they do what they do because I name them."

Kate knelt in front of Tia. "You know what I'd name you if you were a doll?"

"What?"

"Blessing."

Caleb felt an odd lump in his throat. What a terrific thing to say to a child. And what a difference from the words he used to hear growing up.

"Aww. Thank you, Auntie Kate." Tia hugged her neck and whispered conspiratorially over her to Caleb. "She's not really my aunt, but I wish she was. If you married her she would be."

Kate tugged Tia to face her. "Oh, Tia, we're not each other's type. So, sweetie, that won't happen, okay?"

"That's what my daddy and Bri said for a while, too, and now they're gettin' *marrrried,*" Tia said in a sing-song voice while prancing on tiptoes.

"Well," Caleb jumped in. "Are you about ready to get dressed? We're going out to eat somewhere nice."

"Yummy!" Tia clapped. As Caleb pulled out a new sequined silver tutu adorned with pink flowers, she gasped. "For *meeee?*"

"Well, I don't think it's Kate's size, it's not my style and Mistletoe would have it as a snack, so yep. Looks like it's yours." He pulled a crown from the bag, too. "I have it on good authority you're a princess."

"I am. I really, really am." Tia exhaled pure delight.

Tia slipped the tutu over her jeans. Caleb knelt and

set the fancy tiara atop her ringlet curls and secured it with sterling-silver pins.

Kate blinked. "Mercy, Caleb. That looks expensive!"

"Yeah, well. I won't always be around. I want her to remember me after I'm gone."

Tia froze, burst into tears and ran to her room.

The door slammed. Caleb stared at it, his face blank and blinking. "Wow. Man. What did I say?"

Kate rose. "That you wouldn't always be around. She knows being overseas is dangerous, Caleb."

"I feel like a jerk. How do I fix this?"

"Don't go to ranger school?"

His jaw clenched. "Next answer."

"I'll go talk to her. You need to come with me, though."

Tia had her own room for all of her things—and that was where they found her. Since Bri had babysat Tia before she and Ian got engaged, that's where most of Tia's toys and clothes had accumulated, including Mistletoe, Miss Jonah and the trillion other dolls Tia hoarded.

Once there, Caleb gently pulled Tia onto his knee. "I'm really sorry, T. I didn't mean to scare you and make you cry."

"Well you *did*. I hate the army! It made my mom leave my dad and me and it made my dad sad and it's taking you away forever!"

"Not forever. Just for a little while."

She straightened. "How long is a little while?"

"A few years. Five, ten maybe?"

"Five or *ten!*" She flung herself back onto the bed. "That's horrible, Uncle C!"

He tugged her up. "Then come on and let's get to spending quality time together at a restaurant fit for a princess."

"Giggles wants to come with us."

Caleb laughed. "Does she, now? That's fantastic." He picked Tia up and kissed her cheek. "Kate's right. From now on, you, miss fearless dolly leader, shall be called Princess Blessing."

He reached for the doll he thought was Giggles. By now they all sort of ran together. "C'mon, Miss Giggles. Time to eat."

"Uncle C, that's not her. This doll don't got a name yet. My mom got her for me. First present she ever got me."

"In that case, I think you should name her Hope."

"What for?" Tia scowled. "I got Bri now to be my mom."

"Because you never know how God will work in your real mom's heart. Hope a little. Okay? If she won't let God bring her to it, he'll bring you through it." Caleb hugged her again.

"'Kay." She hugged the matted-haired fairy, adorned with Sharpie bracelets. "Welcome to your naming ceramics, Hope."

"Ceremony. And to celebrate, everyone gets dessert at GT."

Ten steps into Golden T, Caleb realized why Kate tried to steer him clear. "Oops." He grinned at Kate's pursed lips and stiff demeanor beside him. Clearly, this was a romantic joint. Famous movie couples graced walls. Rose and Jack on the bow of the *Titanic*. Next to them, *Gone with the Wind, Phantom of the Opera* and *Pride and Prejudice* marquees.

Golden T's wallpaper consisted entirely of sweet romance novel covers. Everything in the place blared romance. Cupid lamps. Low lighting. Pink satin tablecloths with flickering candles and fresh roses. Heart-shaped chair backs. Artsy statues and other tasteful, classy depictions of couples lined shelves.

Classic love-song albums through the ages hung in glass-and-gold filigree frames above the bar area. More romantic movie marquees hung above every table.

Oh, well. He was here for the steak. Who cared what people assumed? Yet, as "Unchained Melody" wafted from the speakers, Caleb's tie tightened around his neck of its own accord.

A text bleeped on Kate's phone. As she read through it, she paled and pressed her phone to her stomach. She looked extremely upset, averting her gaze.

Thankfully Tia was preoccupied with Giggles. As Kate processed the text, Caleb felt she needed the space, time and quiet to calm. He shifted to peer around at Golden T's classy, well-thought-out décor. Unfortunately, the hostess appeared before he could find her a place to go and pull herself together.

"This way," the hostess said.

As they were seated, Caleb forced himself not to freak out when their waitress approached wearing a Venetian eye mask. God definitely had a sense of humor. Caleb picked up the white silk napkin embroidered with red hearts and dabbed sweat off his brow.

Kate shifted uncomfortably in her seat, as well.

"Oh, what a lovely couple," the waitress said.

Caleb groaned inwardly. This steak had better be good.

"Adorable!" Tia exclaimed as she picked up the salt-and-pepper shakers which were Pepe Le Pew and a gal skunk. The sugar shaker was in the shape of the Eiffel Tower. The menu boasted photos of popular honeymoon spots. Hawaii, Cancun, beaches at sunset and sunrise.

Caleb glanced at Kate and hoped she saw the beach

photos. They'd remind her to remember the dawn and that it always triumphs over the night. His gut churned with worry over the text she'd gotten, but if she wasn't willing to offer up the info, he couldn't squeeze words from mortar. He slipped his phone under the table and quickly sent Asher a text.

Hey, pray 4 Kate. Don't call. Just pray. Thx, bro. BTW, I got the job @ EPTC. So thx 4 sendin' a few up 4 me. It worked.

Caleb pushed Send and looked up to see their waitress returning.

"Yummy!" Tia exclaimed when the waitress set down their ice waters and three tiny bite-size chocolate roses.

"You like chocolate?" the masked waitress asked.

"Oh, boy! Do I ever!"

"Be sure to ask your mom and dad here for permission to eat it before your meal, okay?" The waitress leaned in and whispered loudly, "I have a feeling they'll not only say yes, but let you have a pinch of their chocolate roses, too."

Tia covered her mouth and giggled.

He opened his menu and sought Kate's gaze. "I concede. Next time, you pick the place to eat."

She laughed. "Perhaps I was too subtle in my protests."

He grinned. "Yeah. I'd say so. Tia, look. How exciting! They have broccoli here!" Caleb teased, knowing she hated it.

She twisted her lips in a hilarious snarl then put Giggles nose to nose. "Noooo, Giggles! Don't listen to him. Stay *awaaaay* from the Clutches! Broccoli is bad, bad, even when daddies drown it in cheese to hide it. It's yucky and stinks like lake water!"

Kate laughed out loud and her eyes sparkled with fun. Tia had a way of bringing out the playful side in people. If Caleb was still a praying man, he'd tell God thanks for putting such a special child in the lives of the people he cared about.

A deep ache twinged inside him at his lost relationship with God. He may not be heard, but here goes... *Thank You for little Tia.*

The waitress came back with a silver heart tray of food.

"This is our free appetizer sampler." She set it down.

Tia gasped. "Ew! Yuck. That's broccoli! And it's burnt!"

The waitress laughed. "It's grilled in sea salt."

"*Sea* salt? Gross!" Genuinely horrified, Tia stared at the plate.

Caleb pressed a napkin to his mouth but he couldn't stop laughing. Kate gave him a pretty good Mommy Look...but it just made him laugh harder. Kate shook her head and handed a broccoli stem to Tia. "Try one bite. You might like it this way."

Tia looked at Kate as if she was the enemy. "No, thank you."

Grinning, the waitress stepped away. Kate drew breath and held her ground with the broccoli. "It's not a suggestion, Tia. Kids are starving all over the world."

She jabbed a finger at the broccoli. "Then mail 'em that!"

Caleb pressed the napkin against his mouth again. His shoulders quaked. He should help Kate. He really should. But this was far too much fun. Relenting slightly, Tia took a bite—and promptly gagged. Kate pinched off a piece and handed it to Caleb. Giving him a look that clearly said *Set a good example.*

"Uh, I don't—"

"Eat. It." Kate's gaze left no room for protest.

Caleb crunched it down, even though he nearly gagged, too.

The second Kate looked down, messing with her phone as a text came in, Tia grabbed the paper napkin from under her water glass and scraped the broccoli, whole, out of her mouth.

He leaned in and Tia's eyes widened at being caught. He whispered, "Don't worry. I do that, too, when Bri's not looking."

Tia giggled. Kate was too distracted to notice. She seemed unsettled. Was something wrong?

Tia sighed and cupped a hand over his ear. "Kate looks sad." Tia picked up a floret of broccoli and ate it bravely.

He hated to see the sweet kid try to choke the gross green stuff down. Especially when Kate wasn't even paying attention. "Hey, I don't think she's upset at you. Ya know?"

"I know. But I like to make her happy." Tia ate another piece.

Caleb reached for one, too, even though he was dreading this taste.

Tia smiled and wove her arm through his, leaned over and hugged him, then stayed that way, wound and leaning against his arm. "I love you, Uncle C. I wish you didn't gotta leave us."

Caleb's throat clenched in a way that had nothing to do with broccoli being his least favorite vegetable. Tia... wow. The love.

Princess Blessing? Yeah. That and more. As bad as

he'd wanted one of these steaks, his appetite fled at the thought of what leaving Eagle Point was going to be like. He studied Tia, and, admittedly Kate, and knew they'd be two of the hardest goodbyes. Tia could be driving by the time he returned. Confusion and doubt about his decision whirled like tornados in his head.

But he'd been planning this ranger gig all his life. Despite the heartache, despite the tears, no matter the grievous goodbye, he was leaving in two months to return to his unit, whether ranger school was on the horizon or not. He hoped it was. A shot at the fruition of his lifelong dream would be the only thing that could make leaving his hometown bearable.

He couldn't be distracted by emotions or hurt or tears.

It was ranger school, or bust.

This wasn't happening.

But according to Dad's text, it was. They were opting for divorce mediation rather than marriage counseling. They weren't trying to fix it. They were trying to end it. Kate felt sick. No way could she hold food down. Hopefully Caleb would understand. Tia, she could fool. After all, bluffing was her specialty, right?

She felt Caleb's concern, the weight of his stare sweeping her often. She wasn't going to cave and meet his gaze. She couldn't get emotional in front of Tia. It would upset her.

A new text vibrated Kate's phone from Mom. It simply said, "Urgent. Call me, stat."

Grandpa? Kate stilled and fought nausea. She smiled airily. "I need to step outside. Can you keep an eye on Tia for me?"

Caleb's gaze bored into hers. He wasn't fooled, but

at least he didn't argue. "Of course. I'm here to help. Remember?"

His words held a gravity that surpassed their literal meaning. He was sending her a Tia-proof message that he was here if she needed emotional support. She didn't. Couldn't.

"Excuse me." She walked as calmly to the outdoor terrace area as possible. She needed air, ASAP. And she needed to call Mom.

"Hello, Mom?" Kate said when she answered. "Is Grandpa—"

"No, no, Kate. Grandpa is holding his own. It's me. I found out your dad's not contesting the divorce." Her mom burst into tears. "I—I'm so devastated. I shouldn't be. I asked for it. I guess I never dreamed he'd give me, us, up so easily."

"I'm so sorry, Mom. Maybe he knows how stubborn you are and doesn't feel it's worth a shot." Kate winced at her own words.

"No, I guess it's not. I've never been worth his time or trouble, so, while my head tells me I'm better off, my heart is shattered. I've started this and I can't go back."

"Mom, yes you can. Don't be prideful."

"He'll go to war for everything and everyone but me. Sorry, Kate. I shouldn't unload like this. You're probably busy, or—"

"No. No, Mom, I'm not too busy to be here for you." Kate's knees knocked to a near buckle. Her world rocked at Mom's uncharacteristic display of emotion and dismay. Mom was the strongest person she knew. "Did you guys talk about trying counseling?"

"No. I think we're way past that, honey."

"You're never too far gone. Find a Christian counselor immediately and at least try. I know Dad will do it."

"I'm so sleep deprived from everything going on with Grandma and Grandpa, I'm not sure I have it in me to hash it all out, Kate. Counselors want you to talk, talk, talk and I'm just…so tired."

That may be part of the problem. "Mom, don't do anything drastic until after Grandpa's gone."

"Katherine!"

"Sorry. But at this point we need to focus on what's salvageable. You know the prognosis for Grandpa is grave. It's only a matter of time. Your marriage can still be saved."

A soft intake of air then a muffled sob sounded. Like maybe her mom desperately wanted to hear that and have it be possible.

"Mom, you're beyond tired right now. You know what severe and prolonged sleep deprivation can do to a person emotionally, physiologically and mentally. So I ask with all my heart, don't do or say or sign *anything* else pertaining to your divorce right now. Please? For me? That's all I'll ever ask you for. Please, Mom. I am begging."

"That doesn't become you, Kate. Being strong means never having to beg."

"Fine, then I'm weak. I want my family, Mom, and I'm willing to beg for it."

"You'll still have us. Just in a different capacity."

"No. It's not the same. It won't be the same. I want us together. Please, try." Kate's throat tightened, eyes burned.

Then she felt a presence stir behind her and she whirled, half expecting to see the bandit. But it was just Caleb. Kate covered the phone, hating how annoyed she felt at his intrusion. Yet the concern in his gorgeous eyes became her undoing. She muted the phone, resisting the urge to yell, "What?" but tapered her reaction to an even, "May I help you, Landis?"

"I wish you'd really mean that, Kate. Because I'd love nothing more than to help you." He nodded to the phone. "Everything okay? Obviously not. What's going on? Be real."

"No, things are not okay, and since I'm not sure they'll ever be, there's no use hashing it out."

Kate froze. She'd uttered Mother's very words. She stood like that, stunned, clutching the muted phone. A knot sat in her throat the size of a rock. Forget it, she was the rock.

And for the first time in her life, she realized that might not always be a good thing.

Her life and future flashed before her eyes and she had a sinking sensation she'd never find love. Just as BB had said. If she focused on staying strong and not letting herself be open to hurt, she'd close herself off to happiness, too. And love.

Caleb reached over, took the phone from her hands, switched off the mute setting and said, "Hi, I'm not sure who this is, but Kate needs to call you back."

Kate blinked at Caleb then angled her head. Why could she not rip her eyes away from him? His eyebrows raised as her mom chattered on the other line. "Who am I? Caleb Landis, a friend of Kate's. Yes, Bri's brother. I got in a couple months ago." He stepped away from Kate and eyed her selectively. "Yeah. She is. I will. Yeah, I will. Not a prob. I will. Take care. 'Bye."

Kate rushed him. "What'd she say? Did she order you to keep tabs on me? Because I don't need a keeper. You hover enough."

Rather than seem put off, Caleb grinned. "You're

just like her. Down to the voice and the stubborn self-sufficient will."

Kate blinked. "I don't know what you mean."

"And there may lie much of the problem. Come on, Tia needs to use the restroom, which is why I came out here to get you. I don't really feel comfortable taking her. The waitress is watching her until I return."

"Oh! Sorry. Let's go." As they returned, Tia had three Golden Terrace waitresses, one hostess and two waiters held in rapt attention at the table as she displayed Giggles, Dance, Hope, Shine and a few other dolls Caleb had not met.

"How did you smuggle these guys in?" Kate helped Tia from her chair and indicated the dolls.

Tia unashamedly aimed a finger at Kate's purse. "Why, that big ol' suitcase of yours. I dumped all your junk out of it and put my dollies in there. It said Coach. And they fit!"

Kate's eyes bugged. "Tia! You dumped all my stuff out? Even my wallet?" Thankfully Kate always carried her phone in her pocket. "This isn't a suitcase. It's a designer bag, a gift from my g-grandpa." Kate smiled. "And Grandpa would definitely approve of it being converted to a princess carriage this evening."

Tia's eyes widened. "But it's from your grandpa."

Kate bent and brushed hair off Tia's forehead. Staff that had caught the tender exchange ebbed back into work. The trio had come early, so other dinner guests were just arriving at other tables. "You constantly give your toys and things away to the less fortunate. You'd be the perfect princess, Tia. You have a generous heart. In fact, from now on, your name is officially Princess Blessing. Ready for the restroom?"

"Yes, ma'am! Princess Blessing is ready!" Tia picked

Giggles off the menu she'd used as a flying carpet. Kate's gaze fell on a menu photo of a gorgeous sunrise peeking through a dusky dawn.

She blinked. Leaned in. Viewed the photos on other tables' menus then theirs and realized those at their table were entirely all sunrises or sunsets. *Remember the dawn.*

How in the world had God orchestrated everything to the crux of this moment? How? It was no accident, nor coincidence they'd been seated at the only table bearing sunrise menus. Kate closed her eyes. "I don't know how You managed this. But thank You."

Tia gave her a funny look, and Caleb dipped his head and smiled. He distracted Tia with a verbal *I Spy* game they must have started when she'd gone out to the terrace.

This entire night had God's hand and signature scrolled lovingly across it. And Kate had a feeling tomorrow's sunrise would be beautiful regardless of her parents' choices. God was aware. He cared. He was working behind the scenes. Her parents' marriage and Kate's entire unstable, unsteady limping life were in good hands, the hands of the Great Physician.

Hang in, sweetness. Darkness never defeats the dawn.

Kate's spirits lightened and lifted immediately.

She shuffled Tia into a stall then waited on the powder room sofa. She prayed so no one but One could hear, "I don't know who he is, this stealthy bandit, but You're no doubt using him in my life to keep me sane while my parents blow up their marriage. Wherever he is tonight, bless him. Thanks for Caleb, Tia and even Giggles and Pepe Le Pew. Thank You for making sure I didn't have to face tonight's hard news alone. Thank You."

Kate exited the stall and washed her hands beside a grinning Tia who was way past washing and more into playing finger puppets in the water stream now.

Kate grinned inwardly and pretended not to notice.

As the water flowed over her hands, equal rivulets of peace washed over her. Peace incongruent with her life circumstance.

She decided she needed to leave the bandit a note, for no other reason than to thank him. If he never sent another note, he'd gotten her through today.

Chapter Eight

"Need help?" Caleb asked, leaning against the kitchen counter, enjoying the Saturday-morning scent and sizzle of bacon frying. He waved at Tia, watching cartoons.

Kate smiled. "Nah, I'm good. You can keep me company if you want, though." She yawned, eyes still appearing tired.

"Sure. D'ju sleep okay?" He realized last night, claiming the couch as Kate put Tia to bed, that his being in the cabin might make Kate uncomfortable.

"I slept fine. Your bed's comfy. I'm just not awake yet." She looked at him through gorgeous eyelashes. "Although, I admit I found it odd Mr. Macho Army Medic sleeps on pink sheets."

He blushed. "By accident only. I threw white sheets in the washer for you, not realizing Bri had new red towels in there, too."

Kate laughed. "Thanks for washing them, though. And the mattress topper is so thick and luscious."

Kinda like Kate's hair, even in the morning. He smiled and helped her crack eggs then slide the contents into a bowl. "Yeah, I wish I could take it to Syria with me." He grinned. "But the duvet won't fit in my rucksack."

She giggled. "Syria. Wow. Sounds dangerous."

Caleb laughed because, rather than look fearful for him or worried, her eyes sparkled with glee and light envy. The military had been a big part of her life. Caleb guessed it was only natural that even after she left it behind, she still felt some nostalgia for the excitement and adventure. "You're a good soldier, Kate. There and here."

"Yep. That's me. Soldier on." Sarcasm hit her tone.

He poured the eggs into a pan she heated and she dropped chunks of the cooked and crispy bacon into it. "Cheese?"

"Oh, yeah." She sprinkled it in liberally. "Bring it on."

"That's my girl." Caleb scowled at his own words, but since Kate didn't seem to pick up on them, he let it go.

"So what's the plan for the day?" Kate turned the stove off. Caleb buttered toast that popped up.

"It's supposed to be nice outside," Caleb replied. "I was thinking we could take Tia and Mistletoe to Eagle Point Park to play soccer."

"That'll be good. Tia loves it and I need the exercise."

"You need to go run or anything? I can watch T."

"Nah. I only run every other day and today's not my day." They called Tia to the table and Caleb bowed his head as Kate said grace. Her humble, gracious words reminded him of his mother's, right at this table, a lifetime before her death.

He cleared his throat as they started eating. "Thanks for...making breakfast. Eagle Point's the only place I get home-cooked meals." Man, he'd miss them.

Caleb found it hard to tear his thoughts from reasons it would be nice to stay. He immediately thought of Kate. His gaze found her and for a split second he wondered if he'd have a shot if he decided not to reenlist. Then he quickly came to his senses.

He got a text from Brock asking where he was. Caleb didn't want to text at the table. Breakfast-time should be family time. Not that Tia and Kate were family, but still. Mealtime reminded him of the hours of connecting and lively discussion.

"Meals were always Mom's favorite part of the day."

Kate smiled. "Bri said she used to hate when your mom would force you guys to say something nice about everyone at the table before she'd let you eat dessert."

"Yeah, pure torture since she'd set dessert in front of us from the onset." A memory soured his smile. "Mom used to point to Dad's empty chair and make us say something nice about him, too."

"Even after he abandoned you guys?"

"Especially after that. She didn't want our hearts to get bitter." He set his fork down, no longer hungry. "I'm not sure her tactic worked."

Kate observed Caleb silently, head tilted in a way that made him uncomfortable. "So, Tia, how about we go to the park?"

"Yay! Can Mistletoe go, too?"

"That's the plan. Miss Jonah will have to hang here, though." Caleb ruffled her hair while she giggled over his fish comment. Kate still watched him as she gathered dishes, care and concern clearly visible in her eyes.

Regret hit with a huge sense of "what could have been" as he watched her go about domestic chores. He liked helping her and they worked well as a team. She'd make a great wife someday.

For someone else.

Therefore, it would be in Caleb's best interests if he put a swift stop to the curiosity drilling his mind as to the kind of wife she'd be. It was dead wrong for his thoughts to go there. They both knew she was destined to be someone else's, even if she hadn't found him yet. And Caleb was destined to prove himself by becoming a ranger. Love wasn't a possibility until after he'd achieved his goal.

Caleb fought the slog of regret, rethinking and wonder as they put sunscreen on Tia and a harness leash on Mistletoe.

"The dog's as eager as you, Tia." Kate's grin made it really hard for Caleb not to resent that other guy, whoever he'd end up to be, who'd get to be the recipient of those sweet smiles and killer eyes every day for the rest of their lives. Caleb gritted his teeth, shored his ironclad will and forced himself to look away.

Once he got to Eagle Point Park, a whole new set of memories flooded him. Sliding with friends. Doing clean-up with Mom and Bri to help the community. Freaking Mom out by breaking both his thumbs while accidentally flipping over on the swing set in a failed attempt to impress a girl. Caleb laughed.

I hope you know how much I miss you, Mom. Maybe you do. If you can see me, I hope I've done you and all you taught me proud. You always told us to end our lives better than we began. In your honor, and for sis and my country's sake, I hope I am.

"Uncle C?" Tia peered up at him. She'd approached with Kate. "We wanted to ask you something. It was my idea. Okay?"

He hunkered down, smiling into the cutest little eyes this side of the Mississippi. "What's that, sweet stuff?"

"Will you, kind sir, grant Miss Princess Blessing and, um—um," Tia leaned to Kate who whispered something then Tia finished with, "Miss Princess Kate the pleasure of your company at church tomorrow, pretty, pretty please with cupcakes on top?"

"I, well, I don't really go to church these days."

"Please, Uncle C?" The vulnerability in her eyes and the hope vying with fear he'd say no cut through his heart.

"I'd love to go to church with you, Tia. Er, Princess."

She threw herself into his arms and held. "Yay! I'm glad."

He leaned and whispered to Kate, "Will worship for cupcakes."

She laughed. "We'll make you some. Don't worry. That's on the list for today or tomorrow. Whenever we have time." Her gaze turned serious as she watched Tia run fun circles with the dog. "Thanks, Caleb. Seriously. That meant a lot to her. And to me."

He nodded, not exactly pleased to realize that his scoring brownie, or cupcake points rather, with Kate made thoughts of sitting in church seem bearable. Especially *that* church. "I have my reasons."

"For not wanting to go? We all do. Push past them, okay?"

In spite of himself, he started grinning. "You can't not lead people, Kate."

"Are you saying I'll never be normal as a civilian? Or are you trying to tell me nicely I'm bossy?"

He smiled, loving how her eyes lit when he did so. "Both."

They played soccer for a while, which consisted of them kicking the ball and the dog compulsively intercepting it. Mistletoe couldn't get his mouth around it though, which made it hilarious. "He actually nosed a goal!" Caleb leaped. "Score!" Kate joined his laughter.

The moment ended when his phone rang to signal a

new text message. It was from his C.O.—probably pressing Caleb for an answer as to whether he could come back early. That would mean missing Bri's wedding.

He clenched his jaw, frustrated with military life for the first time as he felt it infringe on life's other aspects.

"Everything okay?" Kate bumped his shoulder. "You can talk to me, Caleb."

He shot her the sarcastic look her statement deserved. "I'd have an easier time doing that if you would return the favor."

"Ouch." She pretended to drag a sword out of her back.

"People are drawn to you, Kate. You're a natural leader. It's a gift I believe you were born with."

"I respect your opinion, Caleb." She smiled. "And I love that you give God the credit He's due. You're not as far from Him as you think."

He stared at her, not even sure what to say. Was she right? If people were given gifts, someone had to plant the gift there. "But being a leader means you also have to show people how to depend on others. No one should have to feel that they have to shoulder everything alone. If you don't share your struggles, you scare people away."

Kate laughed, but it didn't sound very happy. "I think I scare people no matter what."

Empathy swarmed Kate
Lord, be with Caleb, whatever is troubling him.

They watched Tia catapult her dolls off the merry-go-round. She went to her. "They're going airborne."

"Yes! Dollies do fly, after all."

"Tia, you ready to head back to the cabin?" Kate suggested.

"*Noooo!* We're not done here." She scrambled her dolls and ran to the slide, shoving them down then following. *"Wheeeee!"*

"Two more times, then we have cupcakes to make."

Caleb grinned wryly. "That ought to entice her to go."

Kate leaned in. "Sorry. Didn't mean to pry." Yet everything in her yearned to uphold him. She wanted to add "just know I'm here" but he was right. She couldn't ask Caleb to open up when she didn't. That would be total hypocrisy. Kate regretted her walls.

Once they had Tia, Mistletoe and a huge stack of dolls secured in Kate's Jeep's seat belts, Kate headed for the driver's seat then stopped. "Here, Caleb. Why don't you drive?" She'd noticed him eyeing it in envy at times.

"Thanks. Weird as it sounds, I miss my truck." Getting behind the wheel didn't do much to lift his mood but that was fine by Kate.

Kate kept Tia entertained all the way to Bri's cabin. Caleb didn't say two words all the way.

Once there, she helped Tia gather her dolls.

Caleb led Mistletoe out of the Jeep. "I'll be back in a bit. I'm taking him for a walk."

Kate suspected Caleb needed the walk more than the dog did. Especially when Caleb ended up jogging with the dog on the trail adjacent to Lakeview Drive around Eagle Point Lake, near Bri's cabin and lodge retreat grounds.

Kate ushered Tia inside. "We're going to make cupcakes but also a healthy snack."

"Not broccoli, I hope." Tia's face squished into a scowl.

Kate pulled out a recipe for the snack they were going to make. "This little veggie scooter is on our agenda today."

Tia squealed. "That is so cute! Let's do it first!"

Kate spread out ingredients and poked a cucumber slice and cherry tomato half into each end of two pretzel sticks, which made two sets of wheels. She set them two inches apart then laid a two-inch-long turnip rectangle cross-bar atop the two pretzel sticks forming the scooter body. She used a toothpick to attach the end of an olive on the front, its red pimento forming a headlight. She helped Tia poke a third pretzel upright in the front of the "scooter." Peanut butter held a smaller pretzel handle-bar to the vertical pretzel in front. "Voilà! We're done."

"Let's make more!"

Caleb came back shades calmer, although the red that splotched his chiseled cheeks proved he'd exerted himself. Since the dog didn't seem winded, she was certain he'd picked Mistletoe up at some point and run with him in his arms. "Those are awesome, guys."

"Thank you." Kate handed him a veggie scooter. "Try one."

"I was hoping for a cupcake instead." He winked at her, making her pulse flip. Kate smiled as Caleb moaned over the scooters.

"These are really good. Who needs cupcakes?" He winked at Tia who giggled. Kate knew the feeling. If this prince had any more charm, Kate and her resolve would be in *serious* trouble.

Ian called to check on Tia. Caleb asked to speak with him. When he took the phone out on Bri's side deck, Kate figured he was filling Ian in about whatever text he'd received. Was he going to have to leave early? Kate suspected so. She hated it for Bri's and Tia's sakes. And a little for her own.

A knock sounded at the door. Kate opened it to find a delivery guy with a gift-wrapped box. "Kate Dalton?"

"Yes, how did you know to find me here?"

"The trauma-center crew directed me. Please sign here."

Kate signed it and eagerly opened the card. Her heart soared. "Wherever these take you, remember God is already there. He is Lord over the dark as well as the dawn. BB."

"That's it! He has to be one of the single guys from church." Kate ripped open the box and air whooshed out. "Boots!"

Tia rushed over. "Wow. Those are some snazzy shoes."

"I know, right?" Kate's joy rocketed when she realized the paid subscription card inside the boot meant she was going to get a pair of shoes from this company every four months.

"Three new pairs of shoes a year! I can't believe it. This is the best gift ever!" Kate hugged them, a pair of knee-length riding boots in soft leather with buckles at the top, in her size.

"Put them on!" Tia exclaimed. She grabbed a boot and held it up.

Kate tried them on and pranced around as Tia giggled.

"I love them. This was so thoughtful." Something hit Kate. She studied Caleb out on the deck. Maybe he knew the bandit? When they'd painted props together for the storybook ball, she'd lamented her inability to afford shoes. She needed to drill him for info. The second he walked in, she rushed him. "Know anything about these?"

He stared at her boots then his gaze reached her eyes. "They're cute. They look good on you."

"Landis, if you know who sent them, say so."

He zipped a finger over his lips. "I'm sworn to secrecy."

She launched across the floor and grabbed his bulky shoulders. "You know who he is! Don't you?"

He shrugged. "I have a pretty good guess."

"Are you going to tell me?"

His expression went deadpan. "Not yet. I need permission."

"At least give me a hint!"

"I plead the Fifth."

"Why won't you tell me?"

He laughed. "Because I don't wanna die before I get to ranger school."

"He'll seriously get mad at you?"

Caleb's mouth twitched as he eyed the ceiling and the walls as if determining how best to answer that.

"Right." She shook her head. "Well, if you know him, tell him it's the best gift of all time."

He grinned. "I'm sure he already figured that."

"I guess you're right. Otherwise, he'd have sent awful sugar-free candy or something equally unappealing." Kate started thinking about all the people in her life who knew of her shoe fetish. Pretty much everyone. She was known for it. "Must be some guy from church." Which reminded Kate. "You're still going with us tomorrow, right?"

He nodded. "I wouldn't go back on my word. Where's Tia?"

"Wiping off her dolls with a feather duster."

"They got dirty at the park, or what?"

"Yes, they were flying like jet fighters off the SS Eagle Point Park Merry-go-round carrier today on important missions."

"Speaking of important missions, we need to get crackin' on cupcakes." He smiled.

"Cupcakes tomorrow." Kate settled on the couch and motioned for Caleb to join her. "What sounds good for today's dinner besides talking and catching up?"

He jerked and looked at her oddly. That statement hit too close to home, domestically speaking. "Sully's."

Caleb grew subdued again. She'd struck a nerve. Or maybe it was just hard for him to eat at this table, which held so many childhood memories from his mom and his growing-up years.

His gaze swept the cabin and she knew her thoughts were on target. Pain crossed his expression.

"This trip home makes it harder to leave, huh?"

He met and held her gaze with an intensity that floored her. "You have no idea how true that is, Kate."

If she expected him to open up, she needed to try, too. She cleared her throat. "So, I talked to my parents yesterday."

He blinked, surprise evident in his killer grays. "Yeah?"

"Yeah." She cleared her throat again, surprised at how tough this was. "Dad's not contesting the divorce. Mom's hurt."

He paused. "I'm sorry to hear that. Can anything be done at this point?"

"Just pray. I mean, you know, if you do. You should."

"I know. I'm trying. I mean, I've contemplated starting to again. I'm not sure He'd hear me."

"He hears you, Caleb. He loves you."

Caleb shrugged. "Well, I'm a little rusty in the prayer department, but I'll try, you know, to pray for your parents. I have a buddy praying, too. Asher Stone, my unit's explosives expert. Because of his strong faith and heart for prayer, he's also our unofficial chaplain."

Kate smiled. "Thanks for that." She paused, then pushed herself to speak again. "I'm dismayed that Dad doesn't seem interested in putting up a fight. People make time for what's important to them. What if Mom isn't important after all? She's played second fiddle to his military career since before I was born. She threw herself into her own career to battle loneliness and, in the process, emotionally neglected me. I got over it. We became closer in my late teens, early twenties."

"You're mid-twenties now. That can't have been long ago."

"It wasn't. To be honest, I'm just grateful we were able to build a strong relationship at all. I know Mom is glad, too, even though she has trouble saying it. She has huge regrets. We can't change the past but we can try to live without accruing regret from this point on."

"It's no wonder you're adamantly against marrying back into the military. I see why you want out and out all the way."

Was he right? Did this emotional detachment date back even further than she thought, triggered by a childhood spent watching her parents lead such separate, isolated lives? The other question hitting her was why did Caleb care to ask? "Are you asking me to confirm or deny? I mean, why do you want to know? Because you like figuring people out? Or is there some other reason?"

He steepled his hands and rested his chin there. "I like knowing what makes people tick."

That he didn't have a more personal reason for asking about her dating preferences made Kate more disappointed than she wanted to be. "I'm glad you understand where I'm coming from and why I have the dating standards I do." Ugh. That fell flat.

"Yep. All the more reason I should wait to pursue a serious relationship myself. I wouldn't want to subject a young bride to the pain and loneliness you and your mom are experiencing."

"Who said I'm lonely?"

He gave her a look. "Be real, Kate."

She surged upright. "Ugh! I'd rather endure the agony of stapling my fingers together with a suture gun than sit here and take these looks of pity from you. It's less torturous."

"A part of me is half-scared to ask how you'd know that for sure. Have you ever actually stapled your fingers together?"

"One accident, yes. Early in my surgical training. But that's beside the point. I don't want your pity. Period. So stop looking at me like a fragile piece of half-cracked glass."

A muscle clicked in his jaw. "Like it or not, Kate, I can't. Because in essence, what you're asking me to do is not care. News flash, Kate. Too late. I already care." He straightened.

"What?" What in the world was he getting at? Cared *how?*

"You're my friend, Kate. Your happiness matters to me." Disappointment rushed through her, even though she knew she should feel moved by how much he cared— it just wasn't in quite the way she wanted.

Ack! When had that started?

She reached for his arm. "Caleb, I'm sorry. I don't mean to lash out. I do that to those I'm closest to."

He adopted a listening pose. It stole her breath because he arranged himself in the same manner as her benevolent bandit had. *Bri's beloved brother.*

Kate gave her head a shake to detach the similarities. But one more stood out for her. She couldn't rely on the bandit, because she didn't know who he was. And she couldn't rely on Caleb, because he wasn't going to stay. Caleb lived in combat boots. And no amount of caring could keep those boots from walking him away from her.

Chapter Nine

"Can we run by my place before church?" Kate asked Sunday morning. "I wanna wear my new boots, but my outfit doesn't work with them."

Tia, already dressed, readied her doll Hope.

"Actually, I kinda like it." Caleb eyed Kate's black boot-cut jeans and dark purple, peasant-style embroidered top.

"These pants hide my boots. I want to show them off and do facial expression recon on church guys who might potentially be *him*."

Caleb grinned. "Suit yourself." He knew for a fact no guy was going to be able to look past her pulse-arresting eyes. She'd done some fancy makeup artistry thing that gave her gorgeous blues a smoky effect and amped voltage of her natural appeal.

Took massive effort to rip his gaze away.

He buckled Tia, Hope and Calebina into the Jeep and drove Kate to her apartment. "You're right. This is a long drive."

"Yes, considering we need to be less than fifteen minutes away from the trauma center when we're on call."

"They're inspecting your cabin soon. Next week or so."

"Good. I will take you up on your offer to help me move."

He nodded. "Just say the word whenever you're ready."

Along the drive, Caleb fought inner tension and guilt. He'd already been to Kate's this morning before his workout, as Kate and Tia slept. They hadn't even known he'd left Bri's cabin.

Once at Kate's apartment, Caleb watched her bound up the steps, enjoying her athletic grace and feminine stride.

He forced himself not to react the moment Kate saw the bandit's gifts between her screen and wood doors. Her back was to him but he could imagine her smile. When she shifted, putting her pretty profile in view, he saw how much his note, stuffed animal and DeBrand chocolates lifted her countenance. Grinning elatedly, she clutched the gifts close to her heart and went in.

She emerged moments later wearing a knee-length bright turquoise-and-brown skirt that swirled around her legs as she walked. She still had something of a military march about her. Coupled with her feminine grace, her motion put a gallop in his chest.

"Ugh. Changed my mind. Here." She handed the chocolate to him and a sock monkey to Tia. "Hold these. Be right back." Kate ran back in.

"Wow!" Tia exclaimed. "My prayer really worked, Uncle C! Someone got her a stuffed animal. And she loves monkeys! My prayers came true!"

She snuggled the monkey, Hope and Calebina in her pink-and-purple-striped lap and informed the monkey he was on doll patrol.

Caleb couldn't wait to give Tia the gift he'd ordered off the internet for her. He had it tucked under Kate's Jeep seat.

He'd be feeding Tia's rabid doll habit, but Kate told him about how Tia regularly gave her toys away, especially to terrified children brought into the trauma center. Tia was a balm to humanity. She deserved a little spoiling.

Caleb's brain stormed. He knew what he was going to do. He was going to name Tia's dolls before giving them to her. In fact, why wait? No telling how long Kate was going to be in there or how many outfits she was churning through.

He caught Tia's bright-eyed gaze in the mirror. "I don't know about you but I'm glad I'm not the one who has to clean up everything Kate's closet is spitting out in there."

Tia laughed. He laughed, too, and reached under his seat. "Hey, Tia," he said, tugging two twin dolls out of the bag. "Check this out. You have Hope. Meet Faith and Love."

Tia dropped everything and squealed so loudly he understood why Ian had concluded that ear-piercing vocal chords were the difference between boys and girls. On the other side of the coin, Caleb recalled lamps or end tables Mom had to replace because of his roughhousing.

"Uncle C! You're my favorite!"

He smiled. "Yeah? Remember that when Ian's brothers buy you toys, I got you all the cool ones."

Tia giggled and hurled herself into his arms for hugs. She kissed him on the cheek before scrambling back and rebuckling. She busied herself playing with Faith, Hope, Love…and Calebina.

As Tia's imagination unleashed on her new dolls, he

listened, becoming convinced all the more that having a daughter would be one of the best things in the world to happen to a guy.

His mind switched painful gears to thinking about how much he was going to miss Tia and her antics. The thought of not getting to see her grow put the biggest lump ever in Caleb's throat. He'd gotten really attached to little T, and she to him. Now he had to break her heart. He wasn't sure if or how he could any more.

He cleared his throat, but the lump wouldn't budge.

Worsening matters, Kate emerged dressed in a different, but even more stunning, skirt and top. He should make himself stop staring. He really should. He managed to look away, but her essence, elegance and faith burned in his imagination.

Halfway to the Jeep, she whirled, went back in and came out a while later with a dress on, this one a bright pink number.

Caleb scowled when it dawned on him what might really be going on here. Kate was trying to dress to impress the bandit.

When she moved toward her door again Caleb held up his watch.

"Fine," she said, sinking into her Jeep's passenger seat.

Caleb snickered for half a block. Tia "flew" Calebina around and so thankfully didn't hear or pay attention to the adults.

"You're making fun of me," Kate said as they drove to Sully's for breakfast before church. It was becoming Kate and Caleb's favorite hangout. He'd miss that, too.

He shook his head. "That's not it. I have a sister, remember? Although she doesn't change clothes as compulsively as you do. How do you ever conquer your laundry?"

"I don't. It conquers me." She gave a wry grin.

"One thing's for sure. You never truly could be a superhero because you'd never be able to wear the same outfit every day."

She blinked hard at him. "Who said I was a superhero?"

Caleb gulped. *She* had told him. But as BB, the night of the patio. Caleb clenched the wheel and grew annoyed with himself for slipping up. He needed to do this BB thing in 3D: with more delicacy, diligence and discretion.

As she stared at him, he tried to figure out what would have led her to conclude others perceive her as a superhero. Work. That had to be it. "I see how others at EPTC look to you, Kate. It's not hard to put two and two together."

She nodded. "Do you think of me that way? Superhero-ish?"

"In some ways, yes. But there are lots of sides to you. You don't fit into anyone else's mold."

His heartburn kicked into overdrive when he remembered another mix-up he'd made between BB and himself—she'd confided the lack of a stuffed animal to Caleb and not the bandit. Would Kate make the connection, too?

"This convinces me you're feeding him intel." Kate held up the monkey. "I'm pretty sure you heard me tell Tia I've never had one."

Apparently so.

How could he be honest without giving himself away? He'd stick with what he'd said before. "I promised I wouldn't say." Not a lie. He *had* promised that to Bri. You wouldn't want me to go back on my word, would you?"

She eyed him oddly but didn't reply. At Sully's he still felt her stare on him, and he grew nervous she might suspect. But he'd thrown enough believable red herrings at her to convince her he wasn't the bandit.

Once seated, she sighed resignedly. "Fine. Don't give up info. I was just hoping if you know who he is, you could talk him into seeing me again."

Caleb had to bite his tongue to keep from yelling out "You're looking at him right now!" Instead, he headed over to Sully's breakfast buffet where he had his first experience herding a child through a buffet line. Traumatic.

How did moms handle more than one child at a time?

"Gonna share those chocolates? I never got my cupcakes," Caleb said as they left Sully's in her Jeep.

She handed chocolates from a bag to him and Tia, then herself. "We'll make cupcakes today after church."

"If the walls don't fall in on me."

Kate laughed. "I hope not, since I'm sitting next to you."

As they entered the lot of Under His Wings, the Eagle Point church, Kate questioned the sanity of her seating decision.

If she walked in with Caleb and they sat together, and the bandit was here and saw, he might think she and Caleb were romantically involved and that he shouldn't send her notes or gifts anymore. She hated the thought of losing the little surprises that had become her lifeline.

But even though she wasn't dating Caleb or anyone else, it suddenly occurred to her that it might be unfair to the bandit to accept those notes, and especially the presents. What if he had romantic intentions behind sending them? Was she encouraging that by not telling him she didn't see him that way? Besides, the opportunity to nurture Caleb's relationship with God and support his decision to attend church was more important than Kate's hang-ups.

As much as BB had come to mean to her, she refused to bank on a future with a fly-by-night phantom. She wanted someone stable. Someone with character.

Someone like Caleb. It hit Kate like a grenade.

If only he wasn't headed overseas. Kate sighed, remembering Tia's lament about hating the army for taking everything away. Before, she might have said her family experiences were her reason for agreeing with some of Tia's anti-army sentiment. But there was no denying that the thought of Caleb throwing himself into danger was a factor, too.

"Under His Wings." Caleb peered at the sign and the Psalms verse as they walked under it. "Pretty cool name."

"Yeah, it's kinda neat that both places I spend most of my time nowadays have to do with nine-one-one. EPTC and here."

Caleb smiled in a way that made Kate think he remembered the words in Psalms ninety-one, verses one through four.

Tia pointed to the sign. "That was my memory verse once!"

"Really? That whole thing? That's pretty long." Kate straightened Tia's pigtail ribbons.

"Want me to say it?" Tia stood taller.

"Why yes, matter of fact, I would. It's my favorite." Kate gestured grandly for Tia to proceed with her verse.

"'Whoever dwells in the shelter of the Most High will rest in the shadow of the Almighty. I will say of the Lord,

He is my refuge and my fortress, my God, in whom I trust. Surely He will save you from the,' uh, from the, um, the froggy's stare—"

Kate knelt eye to eye with Tia, struggling to recall the verse's remainder. "Fowler's snare and from deadly pestilence."

Caleb rested both hands on Kate's shoulders and squeezed, hoping to impart hope by prayer as he said the rest. "'He will cover you with his feathers and under his wings you will find refuge; his faithfulness will be your shield and rampart.'"

Kate turned and blinked up first surprise then pleasure. Tia's eyes widened. "Awesome, Uncle C! Good job."

He chuckled. "Thanks. Although I'm a little rusty on some, I remember that verse well. It was also one of Mom's favorites."

"I never knew that about Refuge!" Tia suddenly exclaimed. "God's *wings* are only a town away!" Tia's hands clapped over her cheeks.

Caleb chuckled. "Actually, Refuge is a town named after God's wings. God is everywhere at once, Tia. So no matter where you are, you can find refuge in Him."

"That's so cool!"

Kate rose and faced Caleb. She was so close his cologne made her forget what she was going to say.

"What?" Caleb's ears turned red but he smiled through it. She let her grin expand. "You surprise me sometimes, is all." They walked Tia to children's church, then entered the sanctuary. Once seated, she eyed him with respect and warm affection. "And I mean in a good way."

"Cave-in or not, I'll die a happy man now. The indomitable Kate Dalton just gave me a sincere compliment."

"Don't say that." She frowned. "I don't want you to die." Kate hadn't meant that to scrape out in a raw whisper.

Caleb grasped her hand and squeezed an apology. She nodded. They settled in and listened intently to the sermon. The entire time, Kate prayed for God's spirit to reach Caleb and cause him to respond. But by the end of the message, it was clear her heart was God's bulls-eye today.

The kids returned for worship and Caleb held Tia through the songs. He swayed with her as they sang. Tia's hands cupped Caleb's face frequently and other times she rested a contented, smiling cheek against his shoulder. By the time worship was over, he'd nearly swayed and sung her to sleep.

He's singing to You. I know he is. Thank You so much for Your mercy toward him. I'm so glad for You that he's coming back. I know You miss us when we stray.

Kate fell into worship. Her smile erupted when "From the Inside Out," the song Caleb loved so much from the other day, came from their worship leader.

You truly are in control, Lord. Forgive me when I forget. In this storm of losing my grandpa and having to see my family break apart, You are my refuge, my safe harbor, my hiding place.

"What did you learn in children's church today, T?" Caleb asked as they pulled out of the church lot.

"I learned to pray big!"

He smiled. "You did?"

"Yep. If your hopes don't need God's help to come through, then you aren't hoping big enough. You can pray big!"

"All right. I'll remember that."

Caleb brushed Kate's elbow with his. "What did you

learn today?" He had a teasing tone, but his smile made it worth it.

"I learned that God will use the most outrageous means to get through to us sometimes."

"Really? Like what?"

"Take the bandit for instance. While I haven't been taking the bandit seriously from a romantic standpoint, I know God is using him to keep me sane and hopeful."

"Really? You think so?"

"Unequivocally, yes. His gifts are literally the lifeboat keeping me from a nervous breakdown." Kate laughed, but did so mostly to cover up that it was true. Pathetic, but still true.

Caleb grew so profoundly quiet, she lost the nerve to expound. Why was he subdued all of a sudden? Did he think less of her for using a fly-by-night friend as a crutch?

Kate still wasn't at a point where she could admit she actually needed one. Even to herself. Crutches were for broken people, right? She didn't want to be needy or weak.

Furthermore, she couldn't get the nerve to admit to Caleb he was right. That she didn't have to be strong all the time. That she just had to do the best she could with what she had at the time. She felt out of sorts, strength-wise, around Caleb. Vulnerable and increasingly self-conscious. His opinion of her mattered more than it should and in more ways than it should, considering they didn't have a shot in the dark as a couple.

Good thing he was leaving in two months because his presence was wreaking havoc with her hard-laid plans.

Since Caleb no longer seemed in the mood to chat, and Tia had fallen asleep in her car seat, hugging Kate's monkey, Kate rested her head back on her seat and prayed.

BB truly is a blessing but I'm getting confused where Caleb's concerned. You're my harbor from storms; the bandit was a lighthouse, albeit a strangely decorated one. Nicely done, Lord. I don't know that I would have responded any other way.

Pray big. Kate smiled at Tia's words from earlier.

Heal the hurts trying to erase my parents' marriage. Preserve and continue for life all the history they share. I love You. Bless Caleb, too, in whatever he's going through. And, if it delights You, please give me hope that I'll find someone to love someday. Someone who'll stay.

"I hope you don't think less of me for sharing," Kate whispered to Caleb, mostly because her stomach was churning to know why he'd grown so quiet.

He pulled into Bri's drive and cut the ignition. As she released her seat belt, Caleb's hand covered hers. "I've said this before and I'll repeat it as many times as it takes for you to believe." He leaned close and swept her face with a tender look. "Nothing could make me think less of you. I just have a lot of junk on my mind. I didn't mean to seem distracted."

"I know. You're normally a stellar listener. Like someone else I know. So, don't fret over it. I'm good."

Caleb tightened his grip on her hand. "By someone else, you mean the bandit?" He actually scowled.

Which made her laugh. "Yeah, actually. The two of you have good listening in common. And kindness. And humor."

"But you've only actually seen him two—" His eyes widened. "Two minutes or so, right? I mean, you didn't get a chance to talk long that one time you met, right?"

She blushed. "Actually, we met a second time, too. He

was there for me after I'd gotten some more bad news. But you're right that we didn't really talk for long either time. Still, he was a good listener. Two brief talks were enough to show me that. Although I do wish to see him again." She hated that her voice went dreamy. So she nodded to Tia. "Mind carrying her in? I hurt my lower back moving furniture when I was looking for clothes this morning."

"Kate, I told you to ask for help when you need it. If you don't ask for help, you can end up making things worse."

She knew he didn't merely mean in a physical sense, but she chose to take him literally.

"I'm getting a little deconditioned is all, from not being in the military and the workout regime that comes with it. I need to strength train."

Caleb gave her a wry look. "Yeah, that'll solve it."

"What's that supposed to mean?"

"If I have to explain it to you, Kate, we're not as close as I thought." He lifted Tia, conked totally out, and carried her into Bri's cabin.

Kate brought Tia's dolls and her bandit gifts in, still wondering the meaning of Caleb's words. Not close? Close to what? Each other? Him? Close to being able to show her imperfections to people? Probably all of the above.

Was she no closer than she began?

Kate sighed, not knowing what to do about herself.

"Caleb, it took half my life to build these walls. It may take the other half to tear them down. Just sayin'."

The sad look in his eyes caused Kate a level of regret she had never experienced before. Was she really hurting those around her so deeply through her inability to be open about her fears and failures? Caleb seemed so sad at every piece of evidence that she would confide in the bandit and not in him.

For an instant, Kate wished Caleb were him. But, thanks to stupid ranger school, that would complicate her life and her heart in ways she didn't need. Not now.

Not ever.

Chapter Ten

The only thing Caleb wanted right now was for the bandit costume to become cannon fodder. Seriously? Kate could open up to a stranger and not a friend? Still?

Caleb fought frustration and stepped out on Bri's side deck with a glass of lemonade. Nice day. Too nice to sit there and sulk.

He raked a hand over his face then massaged his neck and the tightness accumulating there. He peeked in the door and caught Kate's attention. "If you need me, call my cell. I'm going down to work on Bri's bunkhouses for a bit."

"Sounds good." Kate, looking distracted and disjoined, puttered around the kitchen. Probably getting stuff out for cupcakes for when Tia woke from her nap. Just as well.

Kate didn't look like she wanted company and he didn't have the heart to engage her at the moment, thanks to the frustration of the mess he'd caused.

Kate's head poked out. "Can Mistletoe come with? He wiggled up a storm and scratched the door when he heard your voice."

Great. Another being to say goodbye to. He'd miss

that dog. Not that he'd admit this to anyone, but he'd even miss the fish. It was fun to see the way Miss Jonah circled the tank, wagging her tail fin anytime she saw Tia coming with the Betta food.

Caleb took the dog for a run so he'd be worn out as Caleb worked on the bunkhouses. It worked. After Caleb gave the dog some water, Mistletoe curled up on Caleb's bag and slept. The run hadn't dissolved Caleb's restless energy, though.

He needed to talk to Asher. Or something. Anything to get his mind and heart fully back on ranger school.

What was the deal?

Dad said he didn't have what it took. He was gonna prove him wrong if it was the last thing he ever did. Final answer.

Once outta there and overseas, he'd feel the burn and excitement again. Then Eagle Point's draw would fade. Hopefully.

Caleb threw himself into remodeling bunkhouses and made great progress. Afterward, he made sure his bandit costume was still hidden and that Mistletoe hadn't wriggled it out of his rucksack. Kate had shown up there several mornings to help remodel bunkhouses this past month. He didn't need her finding out on her own. That wouldn't go over well.

He wanted to be able to tell Kate himself. He recalled how excited she'd been to get the bandit's gifts, the wistful way she'd sounded about the possibility of seeing the bandit again. Caleb experienced a twinge of annoyance at that.

He couldn't wait for Bri to get back so he could convince her that the time had come to tell Kate the truth. This bandit gig was beginning to get old. Not the bandit per se, just that he was actually starting to be jealous of himself.

"Dude, I'm losing it." He spoke into his phone to Asher's voice mail after dialing. Finished working on remodels for now, he decided to get back and help Kate with Tia.

Plus, there were cupcakes in the queue.

Asher called back as Caleb headed with Mistletoe back to Bri's cabin. "Hey, Landis. What are you losing?"

"Mainly? My mind."

Asher laughed. "So what else is new?"

"You'd be glad to know I went to church today."

"Seriously? What brought that about?"

"My niece-to-be. Name's Tia. She has me wrapped around her little finger, dude."

"They have a way of doing that. Levi says ya-ya for the blocks you sent. That's toddlerese for thank you. You can't make much, man. I feel bad that you're spending so much coin on us."

"Nah. I'm good. I've been saving money for years." Caleb experienced a sense of loss at not having his own child to shower love, care and goodies on. "I love getting the little guy stuff. How is he?"

"Eh, you know. Hanging in there. Trying to. It's hard. Anyway, seriously, how are you?"

"Fair, but I didn't call to talk about me. I'm checking in on you and little Levi. You guys have been on my mind. Especially in church. You really should come for a visit."

"Maybe we will. I need to find a job. It's hard for vets."

"It shouldn't be."

"Yeah, but I did a decade of explosive detection.

It's not like I can use that in a civilian setting." Asher laughed.

Caleb was glad to hear it. "You could become a pastor. Also, do you still have your K-9?"

"Kevlar? Yeah. He retired with me."

"You could always unretire him and work as a K-9 cop. We have an officer here who should be retiring soon."

"When's that?"

Caleb chuckled. "Soon as he figures out he's too old for the job."

Asher chuckled and asked Caleb to hold on a second. Caleb eyed his watch, surprised how late it had gotten and how long he'd been gone. Kate hadn't called, so she'd apparently been fine with Tia. She watched her alone on occasion, anyway.

Still, he'd given his word to Bri to share the babysitting commitment, so he needed to check on them. Dusk had descended over the yard, lake and their retreat center grounds. Tia's bedtime was an hour ago and Kate was strict with it. He started back.

The smell of cooling cupcakes hit him through the open window.

Caleb jogged the cabin deck steps and saw Kate on the couch asleep and curled into a ball. A box of tissues sat askew within reach. Crumpled ones rested in her hands, tucked under her chin. Evidence she'd been crying. Totally unlike her.

Did something happen while he was gone? His gut clenched. Asher came back on the line.

"Listen, I need to check on Kate. She's here, asleep."

"You're with her? How's that going?" Asher asked.

"Answering that would take more time than I have

right this minute, but send up prayers, would ya? Especially for Kate and her family."

"Sure. Remember you can pray, too. Later, Caleb."

Caleb removed his shoes and Mistletoe's harness leash. The pup wriggled with nervous energy. "Settle down, buddy. Looks like they're all asleep," Caleb whispered. He checked on Tia—asleep.

Caleb tiptoed back where Kate rested in the family room. He reveled in how small and vulnerable she looked on Bri's couch. Yet Kate was anything but vulnerable.

Compassion consumed him for her as he peered around at the strewn tissues. Her phone sat nearby on the floor, so chances were she'd gotten an upsetting call or text.

Sound asleep, she shivered in the rare summer breeze from an open window. Goose bumps covered her arms. He shut the window.

Despite the room chill, warmth spread through Caleb as he stood in the quiet cabin where he, Bri and Mom had spent countless hours connecting as a close-knit family.

Memories of how they'd made the best of what they had even when they had very little made him smile. There was always laughter and love, lots of encouragement and hugs. And his mom was never short on discipline, even in the midst of their dad's abandonment. He admired her for that, big-time, now. Although it hadn't always appealed to him as a youth, it made him into a decent man.

Caleb stood in the middle of the rug, peering at Tia's door. He smiled at how another generation had converged on this cozy cabin. A feeling swept through him, filling him with his long-held but pressed-to-dormant desire of having a family.

Love, marriage and children had always been part of

his plan. He just knew that he had to serve as a ranger first. Only then, once he'd proven that his father was wrong about him, would he be ready to settle down and find love. And that made sense, didn't it? Wasn't it logical to push himself and find what he was capable of so that he'd know for certain he was ready to make a life-long commitment?

His father had been a failure on every level, and though he tried not to think about it, Caleb knew he was afraid of following in his father's footsteps. If he could serve as a ranger then he could know for certain that he was a better man than his father had been. Then and only then would he be ready to give love a try. One day.

Today, that day seemed unreachably far away. And for the first time, Caleb found that fact disturbing and unfortunate.

Kate shifted. He peered back down at her. A different kind of warmth spread through him. He'd really come to care for her. Deeply.

Kate was his best friend's sister. That had to be the reason for this raw ache seizing his chest and throat. Right? Caleb took Kate's face in, hating to see the lines of strain, stress and fatigue evident even in sleep. How he longed to see peace prevailing in her pretty eyes again.

Hang in, sweetness.

He thought the words and willed them across the air, in hopes they'd carry some comfort to her. He swallowed, care welling from some deep place. He wanted to hold her and make everything okay. She'd unwittingly detonated every defense he had. As if sensing his presence, Kate curled more tightly around herself. She might still be cold, despite the closed window. A quilt made by Grandma, Mom's favorite, lay draped over the couch, tucked between the sofa and the table behind it.

He leaned as carefully and quietly as possible over Kate, still sleeping soundly and snoring like crazy. Endeared, he smiled. At his movement, Kate made funny sighing sounds, which meant she'd woken a degree but was dozing back. He froze while she drifted. She made such a sweet scene, he tried not to stare.

He tugged the quilt from the back of the couch and pulled it over Kate as softly as he could. As he leaned away from the couch back, he realized he was off balance.

If he slipped, he'd land on her and there was no way around it. It was never, *ever* a good thing to land on a sleeping combat soldier who'd spent three years surrounded by potential ambush.

His precariously leaning angle and slowly slipping socks didn't help. He tried to brace himself via couch arm. All he could think about was the hard left hook he'd get hit with if he didn't restore his slowly slipping posture soon. Stupid socks.

He clenched his teeth and pressed his knee into the couch to restore his balance so he could stand. Unfortunately his knee effectively pressed into the couch front and the wood creaked. She jerked. He froze, a mere two inches from her face.

Kate's eyes fluttered open and she blinked then stared wide into his eyes. Rather than seeming irked or startled, her gaze swept gently, lazy and lovely and pleasant, over his face.

Her untoward expression zip-lined his mind back to the night on the patio and their first moonlit kiss.

They were so-so-so close to repeating that moment now. His mind alarmed. Yet he could not move.

Caleb called to action every ounce of self-control he had to not only keep his eyes from veering to her mouth, but to rapidly restore his precarious balance. He managed to lift away some, albeit not very gracefully. Disappointment blinked harshly across her pretty eyes, making him want to lean back in.

Which meant it was time to move. Like now. Really. Move. Now.

"I brought you a blanket," he managed. "You looked cold."

"Thank you." She cuddled it close, her gaze drifted again.

"It's nice to be close to someone, Caleb. Thank you."

Close? Far from as close as he wanted to be in that moment. *Someday, maybe, Kate. Just not today.*

The odds were insurmountable. He'd be foolish to go there in his thoughts, let alone try. It would be years before he was done with the rangers, and he couldn't expect a woman like Kate to wait for him. Nevertheless, the moment held them and she seemed startled by the intensity of it as much as he.

With more effort than he'd ever, *ever* had to exert in his life, Caleb tore his gaze away from her lovely face, pressed his palms into the couch and shifted himself away from her and this closeness…and the crazy cozy reckless way they made him feel.

Something tiny slid off the couch.

Her hand shifted and he realized she'd caught the slipping animal, the little stuffed monkey she must have been holding. She brought it back to rest close to her heart.

Caleb wished he'd gotten it for her. Not the bandit.

Argh! He was going to end up with a clinically diagnosable split-personality disorder because of all this.

Talk about stressful.

Kate shifted to sitting. "I'm sorry I made you mad."

"When? Earlier? Kate, I'm not mad." Not at her, any-way. At himself? Oh, yeah. Completely. "I'm sorry. Can we talk?"

She motioned to the deck door. "Let's go outside so we don't wake Tia."

Remembering the cold, he tucked the quilt around her but made sure not to touch her or stay close.

On the deck at the table, he motioned for her to sit. He noticed that she left an empty seat between them, proving she still felt the need to maintain some distance.

"Okay, so let's play the questions game. You get some and I get some. And we both have to answer honestly."

Caleb blinked. It wasn't what he'd expected her to say…but if this was the only way she could bring herself to open up, then he was up for it. "Okay. I'm normally not a game guy, but this could work."

He appreciated her effort. If she'd truly be honest.

Wait! That could backfire.

Caleb didn't consider himself a praying man until this moment. Then he became desperate. *Please, don't let her ask about the bandit.* She didn't seem to suspect, probably because he was such a klutzy uncool dork as Caleb. Completely opposite to who he was as the bandit.

"You first." He reclined as best he could.

"First question, what flavor of cupcake do you like best?"

He grinned. "I know you're not going that easy on me."

She laughed. "You're right. Tell me about your wounded faith walk and church experience. Why did you stop going?"

"I used to. Same one you're going to. Different pas-tor, though." His jaw clenched. This was hard. But if she was trying, he needed to, as well. No matter how hard.

"What happened to the other pastor?"

He met Kate's eyes. "He left town, humiliated."

Kate moved one chair closer. "Why did you really leave church? What happened?"

"Because my dad's mistress...was the pastor's wife."

She stayed silent a moment absorbing that. Her hand came over and covered his. Warmth spread up his arm.

He so badly wanted to twist his hand around so they rested palm to palm. His fingers itched to twine themselves in hers. To claim her somehow. A link. A bond that would never be broken. Foolish thoughts, but they bombarded him anyhow.

She cleared her throat gently. "I don't know what to say other than I'm sorry it happened to you and your family."

He raised his shoulders, then released a sigh. "Yeah. Me, too. But if it hadn't been her, it would've been someone else. Dad messed around on Mom way more than she ever knew."

Exactly why he was determined to prove himself the better man. He definitely planned to be a faithful husband—someday. Yet staring into Kate's eyes, "someday" felt bereft of the appeal it usually held.

After all, his "someday" held zero hope of including Kate.

"Caleb, can I ask you a question?"

"You can ask."

Ugh! Kate hated that answer. "See? You want me to open up, but look at you."

He peered sideways at her. "Okay. You got me there."

"Does Bri know about your dad's infidelity?"

"She knew about the pastor's wife, but she didn't know all the rest of it. Neither did Mom. For some reason, Dad didn't feel the need to hide it from me. He threatened to leave if I ever told. So I kept quiet. In the end, he left, anyway."

She felt bad Caleb bore it alone. She also felt dismay that Bri never told her parts she did know. If her best friend didn't even feel comfortable confiding in Kate, maybe Caleb was right that her inability to show weakness made it hard for others to share their struggles. "My word, I'm not sure what to say."

He smiled. "That's a first. Mark it down in the history books."

She giggled. "You have a great outlook on life, Caleb. So upbeat, and you mostly manage to find the positive in things."

"Mostly?"

She shifted uncomfortably. "Well, with regard to your dad and his treatment of you, it seems you're pretty driven by an agenda to prove yourself. That's all I meant."

His jaw tightened, but to his credit he seemed to consider her words. "So, my turn to ask a question, Kate. What made you finally decide to leave the military and come to Eagle Point?"

She didn't even need to pause to think. "Mitch and Ian. They'd been talking about opening a trauma center. They said I'd be an asset and asked me to pray about joining them. They knew my heart was to leave the military. I hate Chicago and didn't have anywhere else I wanted to go. So the rest is history and here I am."

"You still have tremendous respect among the military community, you know."

"If that's meant to make me want to go back, it won't work."

"I don't want you to go back. I see how happy you are

here. Well, aside from all the family stuff you're going through. I want you to be where you're happy."

Kate hated that the words flashed in her mind: *I might be happy with you.*

"I'm sure, with your family's history, that it was not an easy decision. I admire you for making it, though."

"Did you know my unit had a saying, 'Kate it up'?"

"No."

"Yep. Because everyone thinks I'm so tough. Even the guys would tell their boot-camp recruits to 'Kate it up.' I think I let them all down by stepping away." She shifted. "It's hard to continually live up to that, though. Ya know? To carry the weight of what other people think of you, when they expect far more than a human should be put to. It's one thing to excel, but being viewed as a prodigy can be a curse."

"I agree you're a prodigy. You excel at all you do."

She frowned. "Not relationships. I completely bomb those." She shook her head and pulled her hair over her shoulder. Then socked his arm playfully. "Laugh. It was meant to be funny."

"I was trying to be sensitive. Relationship failures are rarely funny. Especially if you're searching for the one."

"I'm not actively searching. Just, you know, scoping local possibilities out." She hoped he got the emphasis on locals. There was no denying by now the attraction between them wasn't going away. If anything, it had strengthened. Connection had grown out of friendship. She refused to stop cultivating that. But they both had to remember that friendship was as far as their relationship could go.

Once she found a guy and Caleb left for ranger school, this awkwardness with the attraction would fade. They wanted different things, and they'd both be happier when they found them.

"Caleb, it's probably a real good thing you are leaving in two months." There. That was honest. Right?

"Yeah. I know what you mean." He angled his jaw to give her one more smile that was part wistful, part regret.

She might mean something to him. But she sure didn't mean enough to be able to compete with his long-held dreams.

Kate couldn't help but acknowledge the little pings of hurt the truth of that caused. She didn't mean enough to make a difference in his plans. But he'd come to mean enough that the truth of that stung.

He rose. "We should go check on Tia."

"Yeah."

Still, as she followed Caleb inside and watched him peek in on Tia and took in the tender smile that touched curvaceous lips as he watched Tia sleep, Kate couldn't blame herself one bit for half-wishing he'd not make ranger school.

She was a self-absorbed friend sometimes, but these wayward thoughts had nothing to do with friendship. The one thing she'd come to learn for certain about him the past few weeks was that Caleb Landis was a guy any girl could fall hard for. She needed to be sure she didn't make herself susceptible to his many charms.

He might call himself dorky, but Kate couldn't disagree more. He was a hero in every sense of the word and a man any woman would be proud to call her own. If the army hadn't beaten her to his heart, she'd enlist everything she had into loving him. A guy like that? Yeah. Totally worth the risk.

Too bad she wasn't going to get to be the girl to take it.

Chapter Eleven

"Tia, did you do this?" Kate indicated a frilly pink blanket Caleb was wrapped in like a burrito on Monday morning.

Tia angled the same way Kate did to watch Caleb's broad shoulders rise and fall with sleep. "He seemed cold."

"He looks cute." Kate giggled, tempted to take a picture.

Caleb stirred. Breathing pattern hitched, he flipped like a pancake on the couch to face them. Forced blinks told Kate he was attempting wakefulness. A slow grin spread across his face as he took in his two admirers. "G'mornin', ladies."

"Cute, Landis. Although hot pink doesn't quite suit you."

He looked at the blanket, shrugged and grinned. It pleased Tia that he wasn't a bit embarrassed. He stretched and rose, smoothing his rumpled T-shirt. "Wha' time're Bri and Ian back today?"

"Noon-ish they said. Wanna go for breakfast at Sully's?"

Caleb started folding blankets. "Great minds think alike."

It weirded Kate out that in a few days they'd fashioned a comfortable routine. Almost like a family.

Urgh! Her brain was working against her again. Noon could not get here soon enough.

She hoped Caleb would shave, because last night's five-o'clock shadow looked even better at 7:00 a.m.—which was actually late for him to be getting up. "Were you awake around four?" She could've sworn she'd heard him up and around then.

He shrugged. "Yeah. I go work out then come back. Ready?"

"Sure." Kate noticed he was avoiding eye contact. "I don't have a problem with you leaving. That is to say, leaving from here while we're watching Tia."

"So, you have a problem with me leaving in general?"

She pulled her purse over her shoulder and kept an eye on Tia, gathering dolls to take along. "To go to Syria? I do, yes."

Caleb stayed quiet and introspective all the way to town.

While more talkative, he was still subdued as the trio ate breakfast at Sully's. What was going on in that mind of his?

He looked to be struggling a bit, but with what? Thoughts of leaving? Had her answer made him uncomfortable?

After leaving Sully's diner and on the way to Kate's Jeep, Tia skipped close. "Uncle C and Auntie K, will you take me to buy food for Miss Jonah? I have my own money."

"Sure. But you don't need to spend your allowance on it. I'll pay for the food."

Tia grinned at Caleb with extreme adoration.

He eyed Kate. "You okay with us taking a shopping detour?"

"You kidding? Me, shop? I'm in."

Caleb bumped her shoulder. Her hand came easily up between his ribs and arm to cup his biceps. They walked comfortably that way several steps. "You okay, Landis?"

His eyelids narrowed in a distant manner and he peered off. "I will be. Things are just startin' to hit me, ya know?"

She nodded, figuring he meant leaving. "After Bri and Ian return to get Tia, you and I can go have a heart-to-heart if you want."

He paused and peered down at her. My goodness, his eyes were so gorgeous. "I'd like that."

The domestic aura surged when Tia reached up and took Caleb's free hand, making the three of them feel like a family unit on the way into the store.

Caleb cast a sideways glance at Kate that told her their time together was wreaking havoc with his no-dating-Kate resolve as much as it was for her don't-fall-for-Caleb mantra.

Kate tried telling herself it was because they'd spent so much time together, bonding with Tia the past four days. Once they went back to work and life returned to normal, they'd feel safe and like mere friends again.

Kate veered Tia to the restrooms inside the store. "I'm curious why you didn't bring Calebina."

Tia sighed and plucked sadly at Kate's sleeve. "It's because she's in my Bible prayer box. If I keep her there, I remember to pray he won't hafta go. I don't want Uncle C to leave, Auntie Kate!" Tia broke down in tears.

Throat clogged, Kate knelt to hug her. "I know. Me, too."

"I love him," Tia whispered into Kate's shoulder. "Do you?"

Kate swallowed. Did she? "Scary as it is, I might be starting to. But let's keep that between you and me, okay?"

Her eyes lit up. "If you'd marry him, he might stay."

"But he might not. And that's not the life I want. Okay?"

Tia nodded. "I understand. I love you, Auntie Kate."

"I love you, too, Tia. Ready to get shoppin'?" Kate was glad her bubbly persona lifted Tia's mood. Yet Kate couldn't rid herself of the dread of Caleb's departure overseas.

They joined him at the pet aisle. Caleb eyed his watch as Tia decided between three brands of Betta food.

"This one," Tia announced then exchanged it for another.

Kate leaned close to Caleb and whispered, "She's female. She's not only entitled but inclined to change her mind."

Caleb chuckled. "The fish will starve to death at this rate," he whispered back as Tia exchanged the food yet again.

"That kind's the best," Kate said firmly, hoping it was true.

At the checkout lane, Tia reached for a magazine. "Hey, my daddy watches this old show. She looks like you, Auntie Kate! Like a Western princess!"

Kate froze at the image of Zorro defending a brunette damsel-in-distress.

Caleb looked down and flinched. How strange.

"Me? A princess? On which planet would that be, sweetness?"

While Tia giggled, Caleb visibly squirmed to hear

Kate use that endearment. What was wrong with him today?

Kate stared at her apparent likeness on the glossy cover. Tia tugged Caleb's sleeve. "It could be her, huh?"

"Hmm," Caleb said in a singsong voice like the one Tia used. He held the magazine next to Kate. "Same regal posture. Classy dress. Hair, height, grace, build, face, strength and all, just like our Kate." He returned the magazine to the rack like he couldn't get rid of it fast enough as the clerk rang them up.

Kate tilted her head, studying him carefully.

Once Caleb buckled Tia in and they were on the road, Tia brushed fingers over Faith, her doll. "I wish I was a princess for real. For even a day."

Kate asked, "Would you like to be a princess at Lem's storybook ball?"

"That depends. Do princesses have to eat broccoli?"

"Never," Caleb assured.

"Can they ride in fancy carriages pulled by tall horses?"

"Always," Caleb continued.

"The fanciest carriages you've ever seen," Kate added.

Tia quieted. "Do princesses have birth moms who never leave them?" Her chin warbled. "My mommy left me. But Bri is my stepping mom. I'm glad. She makes me and Daddy's life smile."

Caleb looked the same as Kate felt: punched in the heart by Tia's words. Yet, for Kate, it reiterated why she and Caleb would be all wrong as a couple. He was going to leave. It didn't matter that it wasn't for selfish reasons. He would still be gone more often than he'd be home, and that wasn't what she wanted for herself or her children.

"I need to check on Asher and Levi more frequently."

"That's your explosive-device expert ranger friend, right? The military chaplain?"

"Former ranger. He is ordained and applied to do chaplain stuff at recruiting offices where he lives, but they don't have a full-time position. He's a single dad needing to support his son, so he's looking to relocate."

"You should invite him here."

"I have. He's sounded very strained on the phone the last couple times we've spoken. It's really gotten to me."

Kate resisted urges to reach her hand and cover Caleb's. Felt like the natural thing to do. So why couldn't she force her arm to move? Terror. Afraid he'd reject her, afraid he wouldn't. "You have a tender heart for others, Caleb. It's refreshing."

"Thanks. But tender won't get me through ranger school."

"Then maybe that's not what you're meant to do."

Caleb scowled but Kate didn't care. The more she got to know him the more she was convinced Eagle Point needed him more than the rangers. And if Eagle Point encompassed a too-tough-for-her-own-good former army nurse who spent too many of her days crying behind closed doors lately, well then, so be it.

Once home, they took Tia to her room. Even when he put her down on the bed, Tia snuggled into Caleb, which made him smile. Kate, too. She rubbed Tia's forehead until her breathing changed. She met Caleb's eyes. "Caleb Landis, how long have you been staring at me?"

"Not near long enough," he said in a strangely thick voice.

Hard as Kate tried not to, elation broke through in an unstoppable smile. "Every time you break out that killer smile, Kate, it becomes harder for me to look away."

"What are we doing, Caleb?" Kate's whisper cut him to the quick. Not only that, the piercing plea in her eyes made him hate himself for upsetting her.

"Wish I could answer that with something other than I think our collective irrational sides have escaped and are running amok."

That made her laugh. "Not too far from the truth."

He settled deeper in the cushiony softness, and closer to Kate.

She didn't move away. "So, what do we do about it?"

"Nothing."

She huffed. "Duh. I know we're not doing anything to act on it. I *meant,* what are we going to do to stop it?"

He looked directly at her, wanting to be sure she didn't misunderstand him a second time. "Nothing."

She blinked rapidly then shook her head. "Not a viable answer, Caleb. We have to do something if we want this to stop."

"When you figure out a solution, I'll be happy to hear it." He gave a wry grin.

Her phone beeped with a new text message. He expected it to be Bri and Ian, saying they'd made it back into town and would be home soon, since they were due anytime. But her face paled and she leaped up and away.

He disentangled himself from Tia and kept his ears open for Kate, marching in the direction of the kitchen as she frantically punched numbers into her phone.

"Mom? What's wrong?" Caleb got up to follow her and watched as, while Kate listened, her face paled more and she bent, fingers in a white-knuckled grip on the countertop.

Caleb flashed to her without thinking and braced her up. She trembled all over and stuttered into the phone, "I'll b-be right there. Yes, M-Mom. Please h-hug him for me, in case I d-don't make it in time." Kate hung up and drew ragged breaths, fighting her body's attempt at hyperventilation.

"Your grandpa?" Caleb said, instinctually knowing.

She nodded and braced her other hand on the counter. He wrapped an arm around her shoulder and with the other, texted Bri: *Where R U? Kate Gpa took turn for worst.*

Bri texted right back with: *Oh no! On R way. Ten mins out.*

"Ian and Bri are ten minutes away."

"Then, do you mind if I go?" Suddenly realizing Caleb physically held her up, she stepped out of his reach. He couldn't keep frustration from welling. He refused to back away. "I'd rather you wait."

"I can't, Caleb. The Chicago suburb where they are is four hours away. He might not have that much time." She coughed, probably to hide the emotion thickening her voice. Her body quivered fiercely.

"Kate, you can't drive. Not in this state."

"Then what do you suggest? The bus and train take forever."

"I'll drive you. I can easily have one of the PJs cover my shifts at EPTC."

Surprisingly, she nodded. "If you're sure? I don't want—"

"Absolutely. It's not an infringement. You're my friend, Kate. Friends are always there for each other."

When pain deepened in her eyes, he felt like a jerk. Always there? Right. Some friend he was, leaving in a few weeks.

"Go get your stuff together. I'll watch T."

"Don't let her know I'm upset, okay?"

He tilted his head because he couldn't promise that.

Tia was smart. She'd know. Still, he'd never put undue anxiety on a kid. "Go. Pack a bag. When Bri gets here, I'll pack mine."

She nodded and rushed for the door. Paused at the threshold, bolted back, grabbed his face and kissed him on the cheek. "Thank you, Caleb." Her voice choked on his name. Even after the door clicked shut, he stood there stunned.

She'd opened up. A small crack, but still. She'd allowed herself to lean on him, to even go so far as to show gratitude toward him when he insisted on helping her. Granted, she was Kevlar strong. But no one could withstand all of life's storms at once. This one was her breaking point. And she'd finally begun to let him in.

Caleb went to check on Tia. Mistletoe jumped up and woke her before Caleb could stop him.

Tia rose and rubbed sleep from her eyes. "Hi, Uncle C! Want to play dollies with me?" She herded him to the rug in her room.

"For a few minutes. Listen, I know you're a big girl and you probably know Kate's grandpa isn't doing so well."

Tia paused as if realizing Kate wasn't here. She looked up into Caleb's eyes bravely. "Did he die?"

Caleb swallowed and curled Tia into the cove of his arm. "Not yet. But he might soon. Maybe even today or tomorrow."

"Well, it wouldn't be bad for him, just Kate." Tia held up a doll in Caleb's face. "Know what her name is?"

"I do not." But he was sure he was about to find out. He smiled.

Tia tilted the doll back. One of her eyes closed. Tia lifted her upright and the eye opened. "Her name's Wink.

It's what my church teacher said life on Earth is like for God."

He nodded. "You're pretty smart, kiddo."

"Smart enough to know God's clock seems broken sometimes. A wink's an awful long time when you miss someone who isn't here anymore." Tia's chin quivered. She reached for his neck and squeezed. "Uncle, please, please don't go away to those afghan stands. We have blanket stores here."

He smiled. "I'm not going to Afghanistan, sweetness. I'm going somewhere else. There are little girls there, too, and they need American soldiers to protect them and bring peace. Okay?"

"Then, when you come back, will you marry Kate? That would make her happy if her grandpa goes to Heaven."

Caleb smiled. "You are something else, kiddo. But I can't promise anything like that. Okay? None of us knows the future."

She pointed at the Bible, where Calebina rested. "God does. We should pray." Tia grabbed his hands. "Dear Jesus. Please make Kate's grandpa get better. If you need him in Heaven more, though, help Kate not be mad or so sad."

Caleb smiled and squeezed Tia's hand. He summoned courage to urge his own words out. "Lord, I agree with T's prayer. Help Kate and her family through whatever is to come. If her grandpa's suffering can't be fixed here, help Kate and her family be okay with him heading on to Heaven. Please give Kate one last goodbye first."

"Yes! In Jesus's name," Tia concluded. "Amen." She hugged Caleb. "You're good at praying, Uncle C!"

He nipped her cheek with his thumb and forefinger. "You're not half-bad at that prayin' stuff yourself."

"Then would you hate me if I prayed very hard you flunk out of the army?"

He laughed. "I wouldn't hate you for anything, sweet stuff." The front door opened in the next room.

"Tia? Kate?" Bri's voice sounded worried. Caleb rose with Tia in arms and met Bri and Ian in the living room. Ian was somber and Bri's cheeks were flushed. Caleb knew his sister. She felt crummy for not being here when Kate got the terrible news.

"Hi, Daddy!" Tia leapt from Caleb to Ian when Ian reached. He nodded thanks to Caleb and took Tia to gather her things.

"Where is she?" Bri's eyes bubbled with frantic tears.

"She went to pack a bag."

"I'll pack one, too." Bri started to rush down the hall.

Caleb put a hand on her arm. "I'm going to drive her. Tia needs you here."

Relief swarmed Bri's expression. She hugged him and clung. "Thank you, Caleb. If I can't be there for her, you're the next best thing." She sniffled and then looked at him more closely. "Although, something tells me it's no accident you're going. Maybe you're meant to be the first best thing."

Caleb stood with his mouth open but no retort or refutation would surface. He didn't completely know what Bri was getting at and frankly didn't have the mental capacity to ponder it. Yet.

"I'm going to pack a bag. Be back in five. Don't let Kate leave without me. I mean it. Take her keys if she tries to take off without me. She's in no shape to drive." He knew once she got alone, she'd be slammed with self-conscious backlash and doubt about letting him see her in such a state.

Caleb dashed to the closet where his cash stash and

clothes were. He grabbed an extra jacket—an army one since Chicago was cooler than Southern Illinois. He sprinted outside to find Kate and Bri having a stand-off in the yard.

Kate's hand shot out. "I said hand over those keys."

"No." Bri's stubbornness mirrored Kate's.

Caleb reached for the keys and put his bag in the back of the Jeep. Kate ran around and threw his bag on the ground. "I said that you could come, not that you could take over and make all the decisions! What right do you have to tell your sister to take away my keys?"

Ignoring her, he tossed it back in and got in the driver's seat then buckled up.

"Fine! I'll take the train." Kate whirled.

"Fine," Caleb said calmly out the window. "I'll be waiting in Chicago to pick you up from the station when your train arrives. Get in the car, Kate. We don't have time for this."

She flung her seat belt on and issued first Bri then Caleb the Stare of Death. It took forty-two miles before she calmed down enough to speak.

"I'm sorry," she surprised him by saying. "I'm not sure what came over me."

"It's fine."

"It doesn't feel fine. I hate this." She sniffed. "Do you have a kerchief?"

He almost reached in his cargo pocket then remembered the blue camouflage kerchiefs she'd already seen the bandit use were all he had. Instead, he handed her a tissue box he spotted on the console. That she hadn't noticed it in front of her proved he'd made the right call to drive her.

She glared at it. "I'm not going to cry. I need to blow my nose." Yet tears streamed down her face, causing her cheeks to redden and her forehead to crimp. "I really hate this."

He knew she meant crying in front of him.

"Pretend like I'm not here."

She laughed and it turned into a scoff. "Like that's possible. Your presence fills every inch of the car."

He smiled. "Is that good or bad?"

Kate turned sideways and studied him. "I'm not sure yet."

She pulled out her iPod and pressed ear buds in, then reclined and covered her eyes with the back of her hand. "I wish I'd brought a pillow."

He reached his arm behind her and produced one.

She lifted her head to stare at him. "Is there anything you don't think of?" A twinkle lit her eyes up some. Good.

"Probably."

That brought a smile. Kate leaned her head back and slept for the next three hours, right up until he pulled into a drive-through.

Kate sat up so swiftly, he rethought his assumption she'd been sleeping. "Can we go in? I need to stretch my legs."

"Sure." He pulled her Jeep around and parked. She shivered, so he grabbed his army jacket and draped it around her.

"This is strange," she said once inside and sliding into a booth. "Wearing fatigues. Brings back memories."

"I didn't think of that causing you struggle. Sorry, Kate."

She shrugged. "It doesn't really fit me."

"Actually, it does." He lounged lazily.

"I meant size-wise."

"I meant you still look at home in military garb."

"It's always going to be part of me. But it's not what I want my life to be anymore, Caleb."

He grinned.

"What's so funny?"

"I've graduated back from Landis to Caleb. Cool."

She tossed a straw at him.

He caught her hand in his. "Really, I'm just glad you're letting me be here for you. I realize nothing I say is going to take away your pain or make a difference about your grandpa. But I still feel the need to tell you it's gonna be okay, Kate."

She nodded. "To the contrary, Caleb, everything you've said to me lately has made a difference."

Once back in the car, they arrived at the Chicago hospital within the hour. Kate grew antsy when they pulled into the parking lot. "I wish he'd wake up from the coma and be coherent long enough for me to talk to him."

Caleb put the Jeep into Park, then reached over and grabbed her hand, heart pounding in terror at what he was about to do. To ask. What if God didn't hear? "Dear God, please wake Kate's granddad up enough for her to have peace he'll be okay, be with You. I…I believe You can still turn this around, but if You don't choose to heal him on Earth, please give Kate a chance to say goodbye. Protect her from regret."

Kate squeezed his hand. "Thank you."

Kate's phone bleeped a text. As soon as she read it, she went wide-eyed. "Oh! Caleb!" Her fingernails dug into his flesh as she grabbed his arm. "Hurry! Mom said he woke up for the first time in weeks!"

Caleb tugged her back. "Kate, wait. Not to dispel your faith but you know as a nurse they sometimes get better before—"

"I know, I *know!* I understand God may not be answering our prayer to heal him, Caleb. But he's answering a prayer nonetheless if I get to talk to him to say goodbye. Let's *go!*"

Grandpa looked pale and drawn against the white sheets. Her grandma was there, along with her parents. They were on opposite sides of the bed, but at least they were in the room together.

Kate approached the bed softly, her throat convulsing. She hugged her parents then rested her hand on her grandpa's.

A blue eye appeared between tiny, slitted lids. His hand rose to brace against Kate's face. "Katherine Marie. My word, look at you. Your hair got long. You don't look like a boy anymore."

"Grandpa, I thought you always liked my short-cropped hair. It was military style."

"I like your hair any way you want to wear it, child. Do you understand? Just be you. If you are you, you'll be beautiful all the time. And who's this fellow. Your husband?"

"No, Grandpa. I didn't get married."

"I dreamed it then. Hey, fella, c'mere."

Caleb moved cautiously to the bed. "Yes, sir?"

Dear Lord, don't let Grandpa say it... Kate pinched the bridge of her nose. This was gonna be bad. She could feel the awkward moment coming on. Even the air held its breath.

Grandpa pulled Caleb in by the scruff of his neck. "Listen up, pup. That's my girl. You don't do her wrong."

"I don't plan on it, sir."

"That's good. You marry her right up and have me some great-grands. I might not meet 'em here, but I sure will be there in spirit. You take care of her. You got that?"

Caleb swallowed. Kate wanted to faint. Or run. Or stuff gauze in Grandpa's mouth.

"I said you got that? You take care of her for me, you hear?"

To Kate's utter astonishment, Caleb's face broke into a smile. "I'm trying, sir. But she's pretty stubborn." Caleb turned and eyed her meaningfully and unapologetically. "Sometimes she won't let me." He turned back to her grandfather. "But I promise she'll be taken care of."

"By you. Got that?"

Caleb's jaw clenched. He nodded. "Yes, sir."

Grandpa's hands relaxed on Caleb's shirt. Caleb tugged the blanket to Grandpa's chin.

Grandpa's eyes popped open. "What're you doin', boy? I'm not a weakling."

Caleb chuckled and rested his hands on the rail. "No, sir. You're not."

"What's so funny?"

"Nothing, sir, other than it's interesting to see where she gets her stubborn nature from. Also that part of her that won't let others help her. Or let true friends in."

"True friends can't bring my wife those great-grands that are gonna get her through the years without me. So get to it."

Everyone gasped. Grandma stood. "Donald! Don't say that!"

"Everybody knows I'm about to go, Diane. Let off, would ya? And turn those water works off. You need to let me leave here seeing you laughing and bossing me around, like always. Not like this." His eyes grew sparkly then dulled. Peace befell his face and his body went still.

Kate rushed the bed. "Grandpa?"

His breathing deepened and tears streamed down Kate's face as she met Caleb's gaze. Grandpa had shifted into the type of breathing that preceded death. Sometimes Kate hated being a nurse and knowing this stuff. By Caleb's expression, he knew it, too.

She closed her eyes and asked God to let the passing be peaceful.

Four days later, it was.

Kate and her parents huddled around the bed, softly sobbing. Caleb stood in the corner fighting tears. His phone buzzed with a new text. He stepped out in the hallway.

It was from Ian asking which room they were in. Caleb texted the room number, glad the Eagle Point crew had shown up. He'd been texting frequent updates.

Moments later, Bri rushed the room and Kate fell into her arms. Ian and Mitch came around Kate and her parents and they swayed in a hug. Caleb fought the stupid tears tightening his throat again. He really loved these guys. Eagle Point felt so much like home, but he couldn't stay. Being a ranger was already the center of his life.

"Caleb," Kate softly whispered and reached past Ian's shoulder, motioning him over. He joined the hug circle. Lauren, Mitch's wife, started singing a hymn, something about chariots, and Caleb's eyes blurred with tears. It had been his mom's favorite song and the one they'd played at her memorial service.

Caleb tightened his arms around Bri and Kate, still softly sobbing. He peered at Kate's dad who appeared raw and about to break as he watched his wife grieve.

Caleb might not know much about love, but he saw it

in Kate's dad's agonized face when he watched his wife when she wasn't looking. Caleb closed his eyes.

Thanks for answering one prayer. Kate got to say goodbye. I know You made her grandpa lucid those precious moments. I need another couple answered prayers. Please salvage Kate's parents' marriage and help Kate not want to strangle me when I tell her who her bandit really is.

No doubt, he needed to do it. And soon.

He hadn't promised a dying man that a masked bandit would take care of Kate. He'd promised to take care of her *himself.*

And that meant telling her the truth.

Chapter Twelve

"Caleb, please! Not yet. Just a little longer. Wait to reveal yourself until after my wedding," Bri pleaded. Caleb looked away from the begging expression that always broke down his resolve. Instead, he focused on the repairs he was making on the bunkhouse.

He shook his head. "It's gone on long enough, Bri."

"She is in a grief-induced depression. Please, one more time, bring back the bandit. The notes aren't even helping now. She's grown immune to them almost. I can't get through to her."

Caleb agreed with Bri about Kate, but depression was a normal part of grief. Short-term, anyway. It had only been a week, so there was no reason to be worried yet, was there? Still, he couldn't help remembering Kate's sad face and lifeless eyes when he'd moved her into her cabin right after her grandpa's memorial service.

"Please, Caleb. I'll take full responsibility." Wanting to press her point, Bri started up the ladder after him to join him at the top. She got two steps in, then paused.

Caleb knew it was because she'd taken a tumble off a ladder last year and had broken her arm. "I'd prefer you not climb it."

She laughed. "True. I don't want to marry in a cast."

That sparked a thought. Kate's reaction to the bandit reveal was going to be unpredictable. She may be angrier with Bri than with Caleb for keeping the secret. Kate was Bri's maid of honor.

He didn't want Bri's wedding ruined.

He'd miss being the bandit in some ways. He played the part that neither of them took all that seriously. So he felt okay about indulging in the kind of grand, romantic gestures he'd never be brave enough to do normally.

As the bandit, he was never tongue-tied or awkward. He knew the right thing to do and say and write to make Kate smile.

That Kate had shown her vulnerable side to the bandit made Caleb want to continue to give her that outlet until after Bri's wedding. He realized the rehearsal dinner was two weeks away, which meant the time for him to leave was hurtling up fast.

Way too fast.

He sighed. "Fine. But soon thereafter, I'm telling her."

Bri nodded. "Okay. I won't ask you to delay again. I promise."

He descended the ladder and got to work on the handicap ramp and railing on the bunkhouse, its last project. "One bunkhouse down. One to go. The second wrap-up won't take long." Thanks to help from the Refuge PJs, the cabins had been completed last week.

Bri hugged him. "Thank you. I never would have gotten these done without you. Families will be able to use them soon."

"You'd have found a way."

"Contractors are so expensive and there's no one local."

Caleb thought of Kate's parents and grandma, sleeping scrunched up for days in hospital waiting-room chairs and washing up at bathroom sinks. They'd gotten hotel rooms, but they were too far from the hospital to be of use as anything more than a place to occasionally shower and change clothes. "I'm glad you had the idea to let the trauma center use these bunkhouses."

"There's Kate," Bri said over Caleb's shoulder.

"Probably here to help with bunkhouses," Caleb said. "Even in the midst of her grief, she stays on top of her commitments."

Bri nodded. "Emotionally, I worry about her, though."

Caleb hated to see worry in Bri's eyes and the empty echoes in Kate's when she exited her Jeep. He was reminded of how distracted she'd seemed the past few nights at work. He was starting to grow concerned, too.

It wasn't good for her to keep everything inside. It was taking a toll on her already, and it would only get worse.

Maybe Bri was right. If she would open up to the bandit, then bringing him back was worth a try. Caleb formulated a plan. "Hi, Landis," Kate said as she climbed the ladder next to him and began helping him replace the second bunkhouse's gutter.

He eyed her. "So, we're back to Landis now? My name is Caleb. Remember?" Had she forgotten the closeness they'd shared in Chicago or at her grandpa's memorial service?

She shrugged and kept working. Was she, too, growing aware of how soon he'd have to leave?

Maybe. Either way, she was throwing up walls. Big-time. Yes, some of it was probably because of her grandpa and her parents, but he sensed there was more to it than that.

Was he breaking her heart? Would leaving her break his, too?

"I'm sorry if my leaving adds to your pain," he said once they were off ladders and finishing outdoor trim.

She shrugged. "I'll be fine. I always am."

He stared at her, debating that. He knew it wasn't completely true, but a confession like that was something she'd only make to BB. How to get through to her as Caleb? He picked up his electric saw. "Here."

She stared at it. "What?"

He shrugged. "Thought you might want to use it."

A minuscule grin peeked through. "You're trying to work your way back into my heart by way of power tools or what?"

Work his way back in?

Man, this was more complicated than he thought.

"Sure. If it works."

Caleb grinned as Kate tugged the safety goggles off his face and put them on hers. She fired up his saw and went to work. He had a tough time looking away. She was independent and skilled, even in construction. Yet to compliment her would only play into her conviction that she had to be good at everything. Prodigy? Yes, but she hated being put on a pedestal with it.

"Kate, you mind keeping an eye on my tools while I'm gone?"

She faced him. "You could be gone for years, though."

He shrugged. "I know how much you love power tools. Keep them if I don't come back."

Pain lashed across pretty eyes. "Please, don't say that."

He set down his hammer and put a hand to her back. "I'm sorry. That's not how I meant it."

She stilled. "Bri'd be devastated if you died."

He watched her carefully. "Just Bri?"

She stared at the ground. Her jaw clenched.

If she wasn't going to admit her feelings for him, he had nothing to work with. He put his hammer in the toolbox. He kept watching Kate, hoping for some kind of response.

Filled with regret for what could have been, he stepped away. A raw, numb sensation spread to his limbs as it hit him how hard it was going to be to leave her. Not just because of how bad it would hurt her. He'd be hurt, too.

Should he tell her? That would complicate matters, right? Caleb wished for an instant he could put on his costume and be the bandit for a while. Because as Caleb, he had no clue how to deal with this stuff.

After Kate shut the saw off, he looked around.

He'd miss Eagle Point. Man, would he.

"So I realized I never really thanked you, Landis."

He gritted his teeth at her use of his last name. "Yeah?"

"You were really there for me in Chicago. Even after…even after the way I behaved when we left here. I want you to know that I appreciate it."

"I'm glad I could be there for you." And he was. As hard as the situation had been, and as painful as it was to see Kate cry, he wouldn't have wanted to be anywhere other than by her side.

And besides, he hadn't done it alone. The Eagle Point crew had come up as soon as they could to offer their support, and Kate's dad had stuck close the whole time, despite the divorce proceedings. Caleb had even had a chance to have a few talks with the general. He was a good man, completely focused on making sure his wife, daughter and mother-in-law were taken care of as the burial and memorial service were arranged.

"I think your dad still loves your mom," Caleb blurted out.

She nodded. "I think you're right. I'm so glad. But I can't say I approve of how Mom is handling it. Dad kept working so hard to support Mom, but she was so closed off toward him."

He nodded, hopeful she would see the parallels to herself.

"Mom was trying so hard not to break down that she completely shut him out. I have to wonder, how long has it been like that between them? How many problems did she keep to herself, not even letting him know that anything was wrong? If my parents opened up to each other about their issues, would they have received help before it became too late?"

Blam! Caleb smiled. Kate was rethinking her ideal that she had to look strong all the time.

She met his gaze. "Maybe someone needs to see me weak to know I'm approachable—to know they can share their problems with me, and ask me to share my problems with them. Like you did with me."

He shrugged. "It was nothing."

She braced his shoulders. "It was *everything*. I had no one to turn to but you, Caleb. At first I didn't like it, you seeing me weak. But eventually I realized how much harder everything would have been had you not been there."

"Hurting isn't the same thing as weak, Kate. You can allow yourself to feel hurt and show it without worrying that I'll think less of you for it. I hope in turn, you'll be better about letting your other friends in. They hurt, too. Sometimes people need to know someone understands the frustration and fear they're going through."

She swallowed, but other than that minuscule reaction, Caleb could not tell whether his words were getting through.

She squeezed his shoulders. "I'll never forget all you've done for me. I hope you know how much your presence meant."

"I do. I was glad to do it."

He brushed sawdust off Kate's cheek and for a second she seemed to want to lean in. He knew the feeling.

He swallowed and did the absolute last thing he wanted to do. He stepped away.

"Lunchtime. Let's go to Sully's. We won't have many more opportunities."

"Yeah." Her voice held the same sadness he carried inside. But putting distance between the two of them would be best for them both.

Wouldn't it?

Watching Caleb walk away to lock up the bunkhouse, breathing suddenly became hard for Kate. She turned to wait at the Jeep. She felt as if her world was crashing in. Mom wasn't returning Dad's calls. Ever since the memorial service, he'd been frantic, trying to save his marriage, trying to get through to his wife—to no avail. Had his efforts arrived too late? Would Mom's heart ever crack open again? How did it get so hard?

Was Kate destined to be the same way? Follow the same destructive coping patterns? She felt she had no other way to go. What did she know about opening herself up—even to the chance of happiness?

Kate closed her eyes. *I don't want to be that person, Lord, the one who lets pain close them completely.*

Please help me to unlearn any negative coping mechanisms. If I have this tendency to shut people out now, I'll lug that baggage into a marriage.

For probably the first time in her life, she really wanted to talk about her feelings, see if she could get a better understanding of her own heart. But who could she confide in? She couldn't talk to Mom or Dad. Grandma was heart-deep in grief over Grandpa. Caleb didn't need to be distracted by her woes any longer. Not when he was leaving to go live in full-time danger. Mitch's wife, Lauren, was wrapping up storybook ball details. Bri was swamped with wedding planning.

Kate didn't know what else to do, how to handle all this angst inside. Who did that leave to talk to? A caped patio intruder came to mind. The only person on Earth she felt she could talk to had disappeared. She'd gotten a sweet note right after she got back from Chicago, but she hadn't had the energy to give it much attention. There had been nothing since then. So much for being able to depend on the bandit.

Yet, he wasn't even a close friend. How messed up was that?

Kate thought again about Caleb. He'd listen. He'd care.

But he might care enough to be a distraction that would lessen his alertness in training. If he was going to be a ranger, then she wanted him to be as prepared as possible for the lethal situations he was bound to face once his boots hit overseas ground. He didn't need to lose his focus thinking about her problems. He'd be a good ranger. He'd be good at anything he did.

Even being a husband. She wished more than anything right now that she could be the woman on the receiving end of his ring. But it wasn't meant to be.

The sadness felt crushing. She needed to pull herself up.

Help me enjoy the time with Caleb I have left. I don't mean to be a pill, but I'm angry at his leaving. That's not fair, I know. But all I seem to be right now is irrational. Help me. It's going to be harder than I ever dreamed to let him go.

"Whoa!" Caleb reached for her arm the instant she stumbled in a road rut. "Kate? You okay?"

She nodded. "I will be."

"Did you get dizzy, or what? Are you sleeping and eating enough? You look like you've lost weight. You didn't have any to spare."

She shrugged. "Then let's go eat. I'm starving."

Caleb got a thoughtful expression. "Okay, but let me pick you up after you freshen up, okay?"

"We're going to Sully's. I can wear this."

He plucked sawdust out of her hair. "Go home. Shower and change into something nice. Let's make tonight special, okay?"

"Only because I like dressing up, and because I got a killer pair of heels in the mail from a thoughtful bandit, will I oblige."

He grinned. "I'm loving the small glimpse of Kate spunk."

"Yeah. Kate-it-up. That's me."

He brushed her arm. "I didn't mean that. Kate, be who you want around me. That's all I've ever wanted you to do. Just act and think and say exactly what you want around me. Okay?"

A smirk curled her mouth up. "Trust me, you wouldn't be able to handle me in full form if I let loose." She patted his cheek and went to her Jeep.

To her surprise, he chuckled and sprinted to her window. "Kate Dalton, was that the flash of flirtation in your eyes?"

She grinned. He settled his hands on the glass she rolled down. "I hope you know I wish like crazy things were different."

She lowered her chin. "I know. Me, too."

He lifted her face and she blinked, startled. "Caleb, please don't kiss me unless you mean to stay. Please."

He nodded. "I know you're right. But that doesn't make this easy. You're a hard woman to resist, Kate." His hand withdrew. He was right. The chemistry between them was sublime. They loved being around each other, even when the verbal sparring peaked. But it could never go beyond the friendship they now shared. Of course they'd continue to care about each other. They'd be in each other's lives in some capacity always because of Bri.

But what difference did all that make when he'd be gone in a few weeks? They needed to get through this current infatuation without giving in.

No matter how short the time she had with Caleb, he'd left an indelible mark on her soul, her outlook, her life, her heart. Somehow, she knew remembrance of his smile on a hard day would be all she'd need to chase the blues away. How had he come to mean so much?

Regardless, until he was gone, she'd enjoy the scenery and memorize every aspect of his face. Only now, when she looked at him, she wasn't so much snagged on the breathtaking smile, gorgeous eyes, appealing chin dimple and strong jaw. Her attention hitched more on the kindness swimming in those curious grays, and on the care evident in the softness of his smile.

Her face looked lighter, more at ease as she studied him. He realized something. *He* had cheered her up, not BB.

Still, she wouldn't quite open up to him in the same way yet.

She'd protest like mad when she realized he was taking her to Golden Terrace tonight instead of Sully's. But he had to take the chance to see if there was a way to work things out between them.

Gravel crunched under their tires as Caleb pulled Kate's Jeep out of the retreat grounds. "One day, we'll have money to pave this. I'll get a raise being a ranger."

Kate nodded but shifted her handbag nervously in her lap. Moments later she leaned forward in her seat, straining the seat belt. "Hey, this isn't the way to Sully's."

Caleb grinned and kept driving.

"Are we running an errand or something?" Kate fiddled with her hair in the visor mirror.

"Or something." Caleb tempered his smirk.

The second he pulled up to Golden Terrace, Kate shifted to stare at him. "Why are we here?"

Caleb met her gaze. "I love Sully's. Don't get me wrong. But I wanted to take you someplace special. Things are heating up overseas. My C.O. needed an answer as to whether I'm in for another tour."

Now she really fidgeted. "What did you tell him?"

Wow. This was hard. But he could be nothing but honest. "I told him if it increased my chances of making ranger school, I'd come back early, if need be."

She looked crestfallen. "But you might miss Bri's wedding."

"I know." Caleb didn't want to think about that, or the pressure-cooked way he was beginning to feel at thoughts of everything and everyone he'd have to leave behind. "But I'm here tonight. Let's eat. I'm starving for GT's steak."

"Ah, so it's the steak you're after." She mustered a grin, though it looked a little forced.

"Actually, that's the secondary reason I'm here. The first is that I wanted to take you somewhere nice."

"Sully's is nice. It reminds me of—" She blinked and paused at GT's door.

Caleb held the door for her. "The military?"

She nodded then stepped quietly inside. The romantic decor didn't bother Caleb as much this time. In fact, he was almost glad for it. Although he couldn't say 100 percent for sure why.

Still, when they were seated at a Zorro booth, Caleb cringed.

Again, the steak had better be good. He couldn't help but smile at Kate, who blinked wide-eyed at the Zorro image. "Wow. Memories swarm back." She pressed a tender hand to her throat, to a sunrise charm necklace he'd left her as BB. She smiled and blushed.

Through dinner, Kate grew quieter with each bite. "Did you really have to bring me here? This is sorta depressing." She pinched off a piece of nut-dusted French bread.

"That does it. You can't be depressed tonight." Caleb wasn't sure what got into him, a little bit of BB, thanks to the Zorro image, maybe, but he got up out of his seat, down on one knee and started singing along with the sound system, belting out a country twang rendition of Barry White's "Just the Way You Are."

"Get back in your seat, Landis. This instant or I will make you bleed!"

He laughed and slid back into his seat, but to her chagrin, tables around them applauded. Even the staff whooped.

"Now do it up right and propose to her!" a man said nearby, which drew more clapping, cheers, whistles and applause.

Caleb chuckled as Kate's face darkened into seven shades of red. "I can't believe you did that."

He smiled. "But you'll never forget this night now, will ya?"

She laughed. "No. I certainly will not." She grew serious. "But if that was your last-ditch effort to make sure I don't forget you, Caleb, it wasn't necessary. You are etched forever in my mind and memories."

"Only your mind and memories?" *Say heart, Kate. Come on. Give me something to work with here. That glimmer you mentioned.*

Her lips pursed. "Would it matter if I said more, Caleb? Would it really and truly make a difference?"

Wow.

That was the hardest question his heart had ever been asked. Because, in truth, he honestly didn't know.

He understood Kate's reasons for not wanting a military husband. But he also knew his own reasons for wanting to be a ranger. The deepest sense of sadness hit because he feared deep down, ranger school was too deeply ingrained to let anything or anyone compete with it.

If he had to choose, could he put Kate over his dreams? That the answer didn't readily come was *not* a good sign.

Kate was quiet and aloof the rest of the week at all the events they shared. Work. Prop building, which they wrapped up. They finished the second bunkhouse remodel in record time. He helped the trauma crew with expansion projects and got them in good shape there. Kate expressed thanks then slogged off, joy stripped away more each day he encountered her.

Time for an intervention.

Time to break out the bandit once more.

Several shifts later, before dawn and while on his run, Caleb maneuvered stealthily in dark clothes to Kate's cabin step. He went to put a bandit note where he'd left others but to his surprise, he found a note waiting for him that said, "To BB."

He removed it and sprinted back into the woods to read it in an abandoned deer stand. He gulped when he read the official invitation to meet again, if only once.

Sensing the desperation in Kate's words to the bandit, Caleb couldn't help but oblige. This had been a long time coming. If it meant that he got found out, then it was time.

He wrote on the invitation for her to meet him at midnight Tuesday on the dock where they'd met before. He grinned as he folded the paper into an origami monkey and took it back to her porch.

No turning back now. It was a done deal.

Would their third meeting be the one where she finally recognized him?

Tuesday night at midnight would tell.

Chapter Thirteen

"Squeee!" Kate grabbed Bri the instant she opened her door. "He's meeting me Tuesday at the docks!"

Bri blinked. "Who?"

"The bandit! I'm serious! Look." Kate showed her the note. For some reason, Bri's mouth thinned and she looked a little guilty. "That's...that's really something," she said at last. "Here, come in—let's get started."

Bri opened packages of wedding-table decor so they could begin putting together rehearsal-dinner treat bags.

"Are you excited about tomorrow?" Kate grabbed her shoulders and squealed again. "You're getting married! I can't believe this. It's surreal."

Bri popped an almond into her mouth. "You're telling me." She showed Kate the treat bags and they went to work. "Ian figured out the arrangement of the wedding party. I hope you're okay with the fact that my brother will be the groomsman walking you down the aisle."

An almond lodged in Kate's throat. "You're kidding?"

"Nope." Bri shrugged. "Is it really that big a deal?"

"I suppose that makes sense, since I'm the maid of honor and he's the best man." Kate's forehead pinched.

"Besides, it's the only chance I'll ever get to walk him down a wedding aisle."

Bri gasped and stood, clutching Kate's shoulders. "What do you mean by that?"

Kate sighed. "It's a sob story. You don't want or need to hear it."

"Yes! Yes, I do. Spill." She pulled her chair around and straddled it, facing Kate. "Catch me up!"

"We have trouble."

"What? Who?"

"Me. I do."

"You said we. You and Caleb?"

"Yes, well, sort of. I like your brother."

Bri bounced in her seat, clearly thrilled. "That's not a problem. That's fantastic!"

"No! No, Bri, it's not fantastic. It's terrible."

"Well, I think it's wonderful that you and my brother are falling in love."

"The dreamy way you say that makes me wanna smack you."

Bri laughed. "Look, Kate. He's struggling with this as much as you are. It's a dilemma. But if you both know how you feel, then doesn't that mean that the hard part is over?"

"He's talked to you about it?"

"Of course. He's my brother. We talk about everything."

"Then you know that the hard part is nowhere *near* over. It's going to end terribly. We can't stop being friends. As entrenched as we are in one another's lives, there'd be no way to avoid each other."

"That's not the answer."

"Then what is? We can't keep going like this."

"If you're asking me to tell you how to stop something already in motion, Kate, I honestly can't. Not only do I not know how to stop it, I quite frankly wouldn't want to. Think about where Ian and Tia and I would be if I kept resisting falling in love."

"This situation is different. He's headed to war."

"Then I guess you are, too. Only yours might be a losing battle."

"What battle?"

"Fighting off the inevitable if you're destined to be together."

"If we were destined to be together, I would not have reason to fight this. But he can't be the one who's meant for me. God knows my fear of falling for a guy with a military career. I can't go through what Ian went through, not to mention what's tearing apart my parents' relationship right now."

"If you're not willing to take a risk for the chance to be happy, Kate, then I really don't know what to say. I can't encourage you to stay safe. Not now. Not knowing how much my brother would love you if things worked out."

"That's just it. Things can't. They won't. We keep this up and we're both destined for heartache and so are our friends and the people who love us. I've got to put a stop to it and fast."

"Yeah, well, good luck with that, Kate."

"*Grrr!* You sound *just* like him when you say that."

Bri grinned. "Thank you. I'll take that as a compliment."

"Bri, this isn't funny. It's serious and potentially heartbreaking." Kate sighed. "Please promise me you'll pray for God to work this out of my heart and his."

Bri's smile fled. "No. I can't promise that. And I certainly won't pray it."

"Why, Bri? Come on. A little help here."

"No. I wouldn't be helping either of you if I prayed for that. Ian agrees. He saw it coming before I did."

"Don't say that. You're starting to scare me."

"Why? Because you don't like the idea of your heart yearning for a military man?"

"Yes. It's not prudent. I don't want it."

"That's where I disagree. Because deep down, I think you do want it."

"Then I'm unwise. Falling in love with your brother would be the biggest mistake of my life."

Bri didn't respond other than to purse her lips in that frustrating way that meant she loved Kate but didn't agree.

Kate wished there was hope to hope for. "How does one know, Bri, when it's safe to hope for the impossible?"

"It's never safe, Kate. But it's always worth it."

Maybe it was time for Kate to stop playing it so safe.

If her heart was going to get slaughtered, it was going to happen with her running toward the relationship front lines, not away. She'd never been a coward, except with relationships.

Time to put her proverbial combat boots back on and *Kate-it-up*.

Caleb couldn't help but feel antsy at the rehearsal dinner. Not only did Bri seat him next to Kate, she'd been smugly secretive about a conversation she'd had with Kate. The only thing she'd admitted they'd discussed was Kate's plan to see the bandit again.

Oh, joy. Could he actually pull this off without bloodshed?

Maybe he should have waited until after the wedding. If he couldn't keep his identity secret tonight, Bri's wedding could turn into a disaster. He would have a tough time forgiving himself if he put tension before or during her big day. But Kate was expecting BB, so Caleb had to go through with it.

God, help this to go well. Don't let the bandit ruin Bri's wedding. Help that go well, too. In case You really have sent this into Kate's life to woo her into transparency, thanks. Don't let me be called away.

Only an hour later, when Caleb stood at the precipice of walking Kate down the rehearsal aisle did he realize his prayer hadn't mentioned getting called away *early*. Just called away. Subconscious slip?

Kate clung to Caleb's arm at the aisle precipice as though doing so would string out the rapidly dwindling time they had left. He found himself wishing for the same thing.

To lighten the mood, Caleb and Kate did the monkey walk down the aisle, which doubled Bri and Ian over laughing.

After the rehearsal ended and dinner guests departed, Caleb knew it was time for him to slip out. He really did have a headache. Probably high blood pressure, thinking of tonight.

Bri was standing with Kate, so he couched his request carefully. "Hey, mind if I beg off? I'm not feeling the greatest and I have my military physical coming up. I need to preserve energy."

"Of course, go home and rest. Drink fluids."

"Will do." He grinned, glad to see Bri smirk as she

gave him the same water-drinking advice he lavished on her anytime she was sick. He was struck again with how he'd miss his sister.

He eyed Ian. At least he was leaving her in good hands.

Caleb waved in the general direction of Kate, who watched him with a concerned expression.

"See you tomorrow, Caleb," she called after him.

He kept walking.

No, actually, Kate. You'll see me tonight.

After taking a legitimate two-hour nap—and drinking some water—Caleb donned the bandit costume with mixed emotions. He walked quietly to the dock early, just as he had before.

At three minutes to midnight, the most beautiful moving portrait began gliding down the dock path.

Wow. She'd dressed up. Really dressed up.

Caleb smiled when he realized she wore the latest pair of heels he'd ordered in her shoe subscription. The remaining subscriptions, though, he'd told the company he'd let her choose.

Kate got to the dock in an elegant party dress. The top was white-gold satin, the bottom a shimmery, elegant black. Replaying their last scene, Caleb stepped out from the shadows.

She stopped. Smiled. "I'm so glad to see you."

He nodded, afraid to reply with the words that wanted desperately to slide off his tongue. *You look so lovely, Kate.*

She didn't make a move to get closer or to peer around the dock pillar partially hiding his face. So, perhaps she felt safer not knowing his true identity. He could hope.

"Thank you for all the gifts, and these shoes—" she lifted a very shapely leg "—totally rock."

He smiled, and she smiled in return, which caused her eyes to sparkle like faceted sapphires.

He struggled to think of something to say in reply, but nothing came to mind. So much for the bandit making Caleb feel suave.

He felt like a total dork, to be honest.

When had he grown to feel more comfortable as Caleb around Kate? When had his shy self-consciousness fled?

"You should know that I've decided your official name is Benevolent Bandit. You really came as a gift in a dire time of need. So, thanks for showing up—here, and everywhere else I've needed you to be. I don't know who you really are. Not sure I want to because that might make things awkward for us both. But, whoever you are, I hope you know how much your gifts have meant to me."

He put a hand to his heart and gave a mini-bow this time.

She sighed. "Can I be honest, though? As much as I've loved everything you've done for me, and as much as I appreciate the gifts, I think the time has come to end the masquerade."

Caleb's heart leaped into his throat. Was she going to ask him to unmask, right there and then? This had the potential to go so very badly.

"I don't feel right accepting your notes or presents anymore because this—" she gestured between the two of them "—is just make-believe for both of us, right? And what's true, what's real, is that I really am not looking for romance with you because I—I've fallen in love with someone else. I fought against it, I tried to stop it, but it was no use. I'm head over heels for my best friend's brother, even though he's leaving in two weeks for good."

Caleb froze. Did she say she loved him? He'd known her feelings were growing, but he hadn't realized they'd gotten so far.

"I didn't expect this to happen. In fact I took every precaution against it. I just…I'm so heartsick because I really don't mean enough to entice him to stay and miss ranger school."

Caleb shifted, feeling extremely like a detonated bomb. Becoming a ranger had been his dream for so long that he'd stopped thinking of it as a goal and more as a clear and unquestionable path for exactly how he wanted his life to go. He never stopped to think what other opportunities he might be missing along the way. But here was Kate, urging him to take another route— one filled with love, family, happiness and *her*. He'd spent so much time telling himself that dreaming of a life with her was pointless that it was a shock to the system to see the possibility laid out before him.

"But he's said a hundred times that there's no chance for the two of us. So how can I tell him how I feel? Would it even make a difference? We still want different things."

Caleb shifted foot to foot, hoping to hurry this along. He needed to go somewhere and think. Somewhere away from her and the truth she'd confessed. Yet hope plumed inside and he needed to figure that out, too.

"You look like you need to go." She looked disappointed, but resigned.

He nodded.

"Well, thanks for listening and coming back again. I wish you luck in your life. And thank you again, for everything you've done."

With that, Kate turned and dashed away as if wanting to get as far away from him as fast as possible.

Caleb looked at Kate's disappearing form. He looked down at his gloved hands and black attire.

For the leather-clad life of him he could not figure out what in the world had just happened here.

Chapter Fourteen

"Beautiful," Kate breathed as she tucked the last pearl bobby pin in Bri's jeweled hair veil. "But you're trembling."

Bri blinked tears and smiled. "It's an emotional day."

"It's your wedding day!"

"Yes, but Caleb got orders today, too. He's been accepted into ranger school. He's over the moon. And I'm sick with worry."

Kate's heart fell through the floor. "Don't think about that now." *You either, Dalton.* She still hadn't made up her mind about how to tell Caleb of her feelings—or whether she should tell him at all. "Focus on your vows and the fact there's a happy, handsome groom out there waiting for you."

"Yes, I'm grateful and overjoyed but I'll miss my brother."

"It was shoddy of him to tell you on your wedding day—that doesn't seem like him."

"He didn't. I heard the guys talking about it in the hall."

"I'm sorry, sweetness." Kate flushed at her use of the bandit endearment. But it wasn't just the bandit's endearment—it was Caleb's, too. That made the flush deepen, causing Bri to laugh.

"What's that about?"

"Just thinking about the bandit."

"Oh! I forgot to ask. How did it go?"

"Fine, I guess. I…I told him I didn't feel right about accepting his gifts and notes anymore. I mean, they were amazing—seriously amazing—and I'll always be grateful for everything he did for me. But even when he was standing there in full costume, looking gorgeous, all I could think about was your brother's smile as he said what your mom told him when she knew she was dying."

Bri raised her chin and smiled sadly while remembering. "That he was stronger than he realized and that…" Bri choked up.

"That God promised never to leave or forsake us and that He's very near to the broken-hearted. Caleb was God's arms for me that day, Bri. Not the bandit."

Bri's eyes lit. "Really?" she breathed. "Tell me more!"

Kate sat on the church nursery glider footstool. "I'm in so much trouble. I'm heart deep. I'm ready to admit it—I'm in love with Caleb."

Delight filled Bri's eyes, then tears. Happy ones, yet she fought off a smile, too. "I'm, uh, uh, sorry, Kate."

"No, you're not. You don't look one bit sorry."

Bri stood and hugged her. "He's my brother. You're my best friend. What can I say? I can't lie and tell you I never wished for this. But you're right. I don't want it to end in heartache for either of you." Bri looked as conflicted as Kate felt.

Kate sighed and straightened. "Well, the ball is flying downhill and there is no way to stop it now, outside of him leaving and me being left to live with the void. I have no idea how to tell him how I feel."

"You need to find a way. He'll have to live with it, too, Kate. Because whether he admits it to you or to himself, he cares about you. He can walk away, but he can't escape his own heart. The care he has for you will follow him wherever he goes. Maybe it'll keep him alive."

Kate surged to her feet, suddenly ill at the thought. "Or maybe it'll distract him dead. Bri, he needs a clear head for spec ops. Not an emotional entanglement. Maybe it's better if I don't tell him at all."

Bri went silent, the way she always did when she knew she was right.

Kate wished she could rewind time and, what? Not have met Caleb? No. She couldn't bring her mind to go there, because frankly, right now, the thought of him not being in her life made her sadder than anything else going on.

"Wow. I'm in free fall."

"I know." Bri nibbled her lip. *Free fall.* Was Caleb? Did it matter? "In two weeks, he'll be out the door and chasing the life he really wants." Unfortunately, that life couldn't include Kate. It hurt more than he could ever know. Not just her, but Bri, too. She'd encourage it, which would complicate an already convoluted situation.

Kate needed to buck up and be strong. Find a way to deal with this.

"It's nothing to worry about," Kate said, seeing the concern grow in Bri's pretty face. Eyes that should not be reflecting angst on this special day. "I'm in a vulnerable place right now. Once I get out of this atypical life season, he'll get out of my mind and heart. Don't worry."

Bri drew a shaky breath. "I don't know if you're right."

Kate braced hands on Bri's shoulders and gave her

the look she'd given war prisoners she'd interrogated. "It'll be fine."

Kate would make sure of it. She was not going to let her struggles ruin Bri's special day. "Look at you!" Kate whirled Bri around in front of the mirror. "You're the most beautiful bride in the world. It's almost time. The music's started. Go get that groom!"

Bri's face erupted in smiles, so Kate's act must have been convincing. Kate stomped all her struggles underneath her surging joy for Bri, Ian and Tia and what this important day meant for them.

Kate succumbed to the joy until the moment she saw Caleb's handsome beaming face; the moment he offered her his arm to walk. "Ready?" he whispered, stirring the hair near her ear.

"Yep." She nodded and just for the moment, let herself feel. Let herself enjoy walking down the aisle with the man she loved. After all, she'd never get to experience it again.

He leaned in halfway down the aisle. "You look stunning, sweetness. Sapphire suits you."

Kate nearly tripped. She stared at him, feeling the wind knock a void in her stomach. As he guided her on, she studied his profile. He gave her a pointed look then stared ahead. Not a muscle flinched in his face. Yet, the way he'd said that seemed intentional. And very much like—well *exactly* like the bandit. But how could Caleb know? Her mind whirled possibilities, but if she thought too hard, she'd faint right in Bri's wedding aisle. She wasn't going to let anything ruin Bri's special day.

There was only one way in the world Caleb could know.

Not possible. No. Way.

Caleb could not possibly be BB.

* * *

He'd taken a big risk with that. But it was past time to
start dropping hints. Forget hints, he was about to drop
a bomb. Not here, though. Not at Bri and Ian's wedding.
He'd do it soon, though.

Once they split at the end of the walk and took their
respective places, Caleb nodded to Ian, who was grinning like crazy. It warmed Caleb's heart and he couldn't
help but smile, too. The guy was crazy in love with his
sister. Ian would take good care of her. *Thanks, Lord.
You rock for that.* The prayer came easily, naturally. His
faith journey wasn't over yet, but Caleb felt closer to God
than he had in years. It was a good feeling.

As the rest of the wedding party walked the aisle,
Caleb glanced over at Kate.

She was still as white as Bri's lovely gown. His statement had shocked her, no doubt. But now her spine was
straight as a rifle barrel. She'd definitely made the connection, but her facial gestures and body language now
told him she'd talked herself out of thinking the bandit
could possibly be him.

When the wedding march cut into his thoughts, Caleb's throat muscles constricted as Lem, a surrogate
grandpa to Bri, led his sister down the aisle to give her
away. Caleb could not describe the emotion and happiness welling in his heart for her. He watched Ian's
eyes glaze and his grin explode. Tia giggled incessantly,
which started others doing so.

Everyone shared the tremendous joy. It brought Caleb
assurance that life would look up for Levi, Asher and
Kate, too.

He slipped into the coatroom after the ceremony and
planted the note in Kate's purse. His last note as the
bandit.

I'm sorry for my silence last night. Tonight, we need to talk. Really talk. Please meet me back out on the dock at sunset. Yours truly, BB.

Hers truly? Not really. Hers, yes. But not truly—not until she knew the truth.

Caleb avoided Kate as much as possible over the reception. She had to have gotten the note because she'd freshened her makeup, which he'd seen in her purse. She'd have had to move the note to get to her makeup bag.

"Caleb, can I talk to you a second?"

Kate.

Caleb turned, making a play of sipping punch. "Hi, Kate. You look nice."

She seemed distracted and waved his compliment away. "Thanks. Listen, congratulations on making ranger school."

"You know?"

"Bri told me before the ceremony."

"How did she find out?"

"She overheard the guys. Everyone is really excited for you, Caleb."

"Including you, Kate?"

She raised her chin. "I'm happy for you. I know how much you've wanted this. Bri will be okay. I'll make sure."

"Bri's not the only one I'm concerned with." He stared into her eyes, willing her to share how she really felt. Her words from the previous night still rang in his ears. *For better or for worse, Caleb is the one I want to be with—ranger or not.*

No words he'd ever heard had stirred him so deeply. To know that he meant so much to her that she'd be willing to take that risk for him made his heart soar.

But she's said it to the bandit, not to him. Once and for all, would she be willing to reveal her heart to the man she loved—the man who loved her?

She stood as impenetrable as a tank.

This was it. Their breaking point. If he couldn't get through, perhaps they really didn't have the future he'd begun to envision.

He sighed. She rubbed her arms as though cold, yet the room was plenty warm. "So, I'll catch you later." She turned.

"Yeah, later tonight."

She stopped, back facing him, steps stuttered…then continued on.

She didn't want to believe the evidence now, but soon she wouldn't have a choice. He'd reveal himself tonight. He'd unmask himself and tell her the truth. It was definitely time. He wished she'd take her mask off, too.

When Caleb arrived at the dock as the bandit, Kate was already there. He walked up to her, seeing her profile before she realized he was there. Tears glimmered off her cheeks in moonlight, causing his heart and gut to clench big-time.

"Kate."

She whirled and didn't even attempt to swipe her tears. Very unusual for Kate. Frustrating because if she knew it was Caleb standing here, she'd be swiping and hiding like mad.

He stepped closer, peering into her eyes, hoping she'd recognize him before he had to say anything.

To his shock, she surged forward into his opening arms.

"I'm so glad you're here. You're the only person I can talk to." Her voice gutted his insides. She swallowed convulsively, speech apparently difficult for her. Caleb held her closer.

"I don't meant to spill my heart all over you like this, but there is no help for it." She trembled, in body and words. "I'm beside myself, bandit. The man I told you about, the one I'm in love with? He's so completely wrong for me."

Caleb stilled.

"I'm head over heels for someone who's going to leave me behind."

What? Oh, wow. No…

"You know the awful thing? Today I finally realized I'd even be willing to consider a military match, if it meant I could be with him. But it's not to be. He doesn't seem interested in settling down at all."

Caleb steadied his breathing. The air caved in around him.

"He's all about the rangers and nothing else. I'm something to him, I know it. I'm just not enough. And you know what? That's been my biggest fear. Not measuring up."

Caleb clutched Kate like there was no tomorrow, as her words sank deep.

"In short, I love him enough to take that risk…"

He couldn't have been more shocked to hear her confession. Yet what shocked him more was all she was willing to give up—like the idea of a normal, stable life and family together. A life and family that he was surprised to realize he badly wanted.

Becoming a ranger was supposed to be his dream. Yet it didn't feel satisfying to be on the verge of achieving that goal. Not at all.

What felt satisfying was having Kate in his arms and confessing her love. The realization that she returned his feelings. There. He admitted it. He loved her, too. So much.

The appeal of ranger school had been fading for a while. Especially in light of Kate. But this moment? On hearing her love for him? All he could think about was what ranger school would mean leaving behind.

He thought he'd find fulfillment in distinguished service—that becoming a ranger would show how different he was from the father who'd abandoned him. But Caleb was starting to realize the best way to show he wasn't like Dad might be to do what Dad truly couldn't—marry a woman and stay with her, be faithful, raise children with her and have a good life.

He'd want that life to let him continue his service in some way because it was important to him. But he also wanted it to let him make a true commitment to the idea of a home and family. In a hard moment of honest self-assessment, he finally realized that that was what he'd been afraid of all this time—that he'd fail at being a husband and father, as his father had, or that he'd be abandoned again.

His gut knew better. Kate was solid. She'd commit for life. She'd love him forever and never leave and he wanted to be that for her, too. Way more than being a ranger, he wanted to be able to spend his days showing her how special she was.

In Kate's embrace, Caleb felt at home for the first time in years. All unsettled feelings shelled off. He closed his eyes.

I'm home to You, too, Lord. Here's where the rift ends, the bitterness stops. It was never Your fault. I'm sorry. Forgive me. Please work this out. Help Kate not hate me when she figures out who I am.

Caleb no longer had peace about revealing himself

tonight. Kate was too emotionally volatile after hearing of his acceptance to ranger school. Also, Bri's wedding had impacted Kate. Her parents had attended, but they sat on opposite sides of the church.

He hugged her once more and pointed to the road.

"You need to go? I'm sorry. Thank you for listening one last time."

Kate, I want to listen for a lifetime...as Caleb.

He backed away and sprinted as fast as his legs would go.

He was sure he'd left her reeling, but that was okay. Ten days from now, at the storybook ball, she'd know everything. All would be made clear. And they'd either have a future together, or she'd have the freedom to fall for someone else.

Chapter Fifteen

"You're positively glowing, sis." Caleb couldn't get over how happy his sister looked as he helped Bri carry in her bags. She and Ian had just returned from their honeymoon.

She grinned. "I had a blast. It went by too fast. And I hate that we had to split up at the end of it, but at least Ian's only getting Tia from his mom's in St. Louis. He'll be back soon."

"Why didn't you and Ian stay in Grand Cayman longer?"

"Ian was afraid of the dolphin that attacked Mitch."

"Seriously?"

She laughed. "No, we didn't want to be away from Tia that long. After the storybook ball, we're taking her on a surprise Disney trip to celebrate us becoming a family." She brushed a hand along his face and looked dreadfully sad. "I wish you would still be here so you could go with us."

"I'll be here."

"For a few more days." Bri looked on the verge of tears so Caleb needed to tell her.

"Bri, I turned down my chance at ranger school."

"What!" She grabbed his shoulders. "What do you mean?"

"I'm not going." He pulled her to the couch so he could explain. "I've been doing a lot of thinking and praying."

She bit her lip and a stunned smile peeked through. "Yeah?"

"Yeah. You know I'm in love with your bestie, right?"

Bri stood and squealed. He tugged her back down.

"Tell me what's going on, Caleb!"

"I'm planning on proposing to her at the storybook ball."

Bri leaped up again and shrieked.

He stood, too. "I'm also revealing the bandit."

"You want her to murder you three seconds after you ask her to marry you?" Bri snorted. "Are you crazy? Not smart, Caleb."

"It probably wasn't smart to do the whole bandit thing to begin with, considering Kate is an M-16 master and third-degree black belt."

"Who taught close-quarters combat to special operatives."

"You're not helping matters." Caleb grinned.

"I know you need to tell her. It's not like we can shove a bandit under the rug. She has the right to know, especially if she's going to marry you!"

"So, you'll help me plan one last bandit surprise for Kate?"

"Yes. Oh, I know! We should let her think you've left for ranger training. Then she'll be certain that you couldn't possibly be at the ball, yourself. She still thinks you're going to ranger school, right?"

"Yes. Everyone but Asher does. And you. I was waiting to spread the word until you got back because I thought you had the right to hear it first. But I'm intrigued with this idea of surprising her after she thinks I've gone— I guess I can keep the secret under my hat for a little while longer."

"Good. Show up to the storybook ball in your bandit costume and end it the way you started it. Plus, it's symbolic since you two helped organize the ball and built its props."

"I like that. The costume that brought us together will cement our relationship." He grinned. "Or my untimely death."

Bri smiled but it wobbled enough to show that she, like Caleb, retained a healthy fear of Kate's reaction to the big reveal.

"This is ridiculous, Bri." Kate shoved the Mardi Gras gown back into her closet. "Why would I wear the same costume I wore at Mitch and Lauren's wedding?"

"Because it looks stunning on you. And because you never know who's going to show up."

She shot Bri a wry smirk. "You mean the bandit? I'm so over that guy, Bri. Don't play innocent. You know the only guy who matters to me."

Bri brushed a hand along the sequined sapphire gown. "Seeing him won't pull you out of—"

"This ache of missing your insanely lovable brother? No." Kate scowled. "Next time you talk, tell him how absolutely rude it was for him to leave without telling me goodbye. Not just rude, cowardly." Caleb's rapid middle-of-the-night departure hurt more than anyone could know.

Caleb's words slammed to the forefront of her mind. Kate sighed, trying to put his advice to practice. "It really stung that he didn't at least call me."

"Well, next time you talk to him, you can tell him exactly how you feel."

"Next time I talk to him? That could be months from now. Years even."

Bri nibbled her lip and didn't comment.

"What?"

Bri's eyes widened. "Nothing. What?"

"That's what I want to know. What's going on? You're acting weird."

Bri shrugged. "Maybe it's just honeymoon daze."

"Right. You're up to something."

"I'm sleepy. Tia was up chatting until the wee hours after Ian left for a trauma."

"I'm so glad you're a family, Bri."

Bri beamed in reply.

"I want a Godly marriage like the one you and Ian have."

"You will."

"You sound so sure."

"I am. You have to remember that love doesn't keep record of wrongs, Kate. Promise me that. Okay?"

Kate sighed. "As stated once before, anytime I've given you a promise, I ended up in a creepy or crazy predicament."

"Hmm. You could call it that."

"What?"

"Nothing."

"You definitely have honeymoon brain. You're not making a lick of sense. Come on. We're going to be late for Lem's storybook ball." Despite her protests, she really didn't have a better option to wear, so Kate dragged the dress out of the closet. The memories tumbled with it.

Kate stilled, remembering every kind thing the bandit had done. But the face of Bri's brother somehow superimposed over her memories of the man and the gifts and it was Caleb her mind was left thinking of and reeling over.

Lord, I miss him so much. Keep him safe. Guide his steps.

That's what Kate would do. Put her love for Caleb into prayers for his safety. And as much as she didn't want to, she'd also pray for his success in whatever he set his dreaming mind to.

"Ready?" Kate asked Bri and Tia an hour later.

Tia whirled in her fancy costume. "Lem says I'm the princess of the storybook ball."

"And what a beautiful princess you are."

"Yes, and I decree my land shall be free of the clutches of broccoli." Tia giggled.

It was contagious, and Kate laughed, too. She picked Tia up and pirouetted all the way to the door.

Tia sighed dramatically in the car. "I miss Uncle C. I wish he was here." But she didn't sound sad. In fact, she sounded like she was holding back laughter.

Bri cleared her throat and gave Tia a strange look.

Bri's honeymoon illness had apparently rubbed off on the child. Tia was acting as silly as her stepmom.

Kate watched out the window as they neared the reception hall where the ball would be held. Townspeople from Eagle Point, Refuge and other small towns showed up to support Lem's efforts. The town square looked like a lavish lighted village, something out of a literal storybook with breathtaking props.

Kate choked up seeing them lit and displayed, remembering the hours she and Caleb had laughed and sparred and shared creating them.

She pressed a hand to her heart. It hurt.

Bri teared up. "All this, for our bunkhouses, Tia."

"Goodie! We can make cupcakes for them all."

"That's a fantastic idea, Tia." Bri took her hand.

Kate's stomach quivered with nerves as she got out of the limo Lem had sent for her, Bri and Tia as a surprise. But why would she be nervous? Her part of the preparations was done. All she had to do now was enjoy the party. And yet she couldn't help feeling that some surprise was waiting for her, just around the corner.

Ian and Mitch came early to help Lem. They'd called rent-a-docs and traveling nurses to staff the trauma center for the evening, to ensure no one local would be called in. Most of the town was here, anyway.

Kate and Bri took turns showing Tia storybook characters. Humpty Dumpty escorted a svelte lady wall. Fairytale princesses strode with coinciding princes. Bri and Ian were Beauty and the Beast. Ian had tried to talk Tia into going as the teacup but she'd decided on the princess Caleb and Kate said she could be.

"The carriage!" Tia pointed to an elaborate lighted one.

"Uncle C arranged to have that here, for you and your friends to ride in," Bri informed, watching Kate oddly.

"A real horse!" Tia ran to her dad, waiting at the carriage for her.

"There's your honey. You'd better go."

Bri stared at her. "You're going to have a great night, Kate. In fact, it's going to be unforgettable." With that, Bri turned and ran to catch up with her handsome "Beast."

Kate stared after her, not sure what to make of Bri's words. She decided to focus on making them come true. She'd have a great night, or die trying. She set to work trying to infuse bubbly thoughts. But in truth, the only kind of night Kate felt she was in for was one that would end up unforgettably sad. There was just too much here that made her think of Caleb, reminding her how much she missed the handsome ranger.

"Katherine."

Kate whirled. Her parents stood in front of her, holding hands. Wait. Holding hands! And dressed like Luke and Princess Leia. They were avid *Star Wars* fans. In fact, a *Star Wars* movie was where they'd met.

"Mom? Dad?" Kate looked from one to the other. Kate's mom smiled and leaned into her dad's shoulder then took Kate's hand.

"We're following Caleb's advice. And yours," Mom said.

"Caleb?" The name slashed her heart like a scalpel.

"Yes." Her dad cleared his throat and gave her mom a sweet look. "We've been in touch with the young man recently."

"Oh. Well, that's nice." *Since he hasn't spoken to me!*

"Mom, Dad, are you—"

Kate's mother beamed. "Here together? As a couple? Yes."

Kate dashed toward them and they hauled her into the best hug of her life. "You don't know how badly I needed and wanted this." Kate should have worn waterproof mascara. Like last time in this patio garden, she most likely looked like a raccoon. Who cared? Her parents were trying to fix their marriage!

Dad smiled. "Seems Zorro wants a word with you."

"Huh?" Kate blinked at her dad.

He nodded behind her. Kate's mom smiled.

Kate felt his presence before she moved.

Slowly, she turned.

Sure enough, there stood her bandit, dressed in full black.

Except for the blue camouflage kerchief bundled in his hands like a gift. She stared at him, then it.

People drifted inside. Some watched from windows.

"You showed up. Did you get invited here, or—"

He grinned and for the life of her, he reminded her of Caleb. Her mind must *really* be traumatized because she was seeing him everywhere. She thought she'd seen him in a jewelry store yesterday on Eagle Wing Avenue. Impossible, since he was in training.

"Yes, Kate. I'm here for you."

She gasped. That voice! She knew that voice—and not from the bandit. Not from the bandit at all.

Caleb? Oh, Lord, it was either him or she *really* needed to be institutionalized.

Her hand came swiftly to her mouth. He took it in his. Tugged her to the corner where they first "met" in these costumes. Kate felt as though she floated in another world.

Once in the dimly lit corner under the umbrella of the brighter fuchsia tree, he took her hands in his.

"Caleb?"

He tilted his head in a confirming nod.

She reached for his mask. He caught her hand. Held it in his and then together they peeled off his mask.

She gasped. "Oh. My! It's you! It's really— Oh! How on earth!"

He grinned.

Gorgeous.

"I was afraid you'd be angry. For the record, I like this reaction much better."

Angry? The thought never even crossed her mind. In truth, there were no words for how she felt. She'd never been more stunned in her life.

Until he dropped to one knee and unwrapped the blue

camo kerchief, revealing a sapphire-blue box, which he opened.

A sparkling solitaire diamond flanked by two blue sapphires winked up at her like hope shining in her heart.

"Caleb! Are you…"

"Proposing, yes. But first, let me explain the bandit."

She dove for him. "I don't care. Whatever the explanation, it doesn't matter. How are you here? What about Syria and rangers?" Her words tumbled so fast he looked comical trying to keep up.

"I chose not to go, Kate."

"But how can that be? It was all you ever talked about! How could you not go?"

He held her hands and stood. "Will you let me talk?" He chuckled.

She clamped her mouth shut, but the next thousand questions spurted at the tip of her tongue and begged for freedom.

"But your eyes, they're black!"

He shook his head. "Contacts."

"I prefer gray, anyway."

"Listen…" He gently steered the conversation back. "You should know I've thought this through. It wasn't a whim. I've even lined up a new career track— I got a full-time job at Eagle Point Trauma Center. I'm also, along with Asher Stone once he moves here, starting an ROTC program here at Eagle Point's High School."

"Caleb! That's wonderful. Can I help?"

His eyes lit. "Your help would be terrific, but I'm surprised you'd want to."

"I have military in my blood. I'd love to help."

"We'd love to have you. Will you, as my wife?"

"Depends. You gonna play any more masked charades on me?"

He choked out a laugh. "Absolutely not."

"Good, because you're lucky I love you enough not to kick out both of your kneecaps, buster."

He grinned. "My sister made me promise to confess she was also an instigator."

"That doesn't surprise me. So, when do we do this ROTC thing? I'd love to head up the girls and you and Asher could head up the guys and for uniforms we could hit Lauren up to—"

"Kate." He chuckled. "Are you going to let me talk?"

"Sorry, yes." She put her head down and stared at their hands. Elation overcame her shock and she smiled up at him. And even though she'd said she'd let him speak, she couldn't stop the words that spilled out of her mouth.

"Caleb, are you sure? I know how much it would mean for you to have to give up your military career. I don't want you to resent me."

"Kate, the only thing I want now—besides the opportunity to finish a sentence—is a future with you."

His serious look forced her mouth shut.

"My reason for wanting the rangers wasn't sound. I've worked that out with God. Also went to visit my dad. While his brain may not have understood a word I said, I know his spirit did. Something about that visit set me free inside. Free to be who God intended. Not who unforgiveness tried to mold me into. Now I know that what I really want isn't waiting for me in Syria or ranger school. It's right here in Eagle Point, with you."

"Caleb!"

"Since you won't let me get a word in edgewise…" He leaned in and kissed her senseless. When she forgot the sum of human language, he trailed his mouth to her ear. "Sweetness, will you marry me?"

She reached for him and clung. "Darkness never, ever defeats the dawn," she whispered into his shoulder. "You taught me that. I love you, Caleb."

He leaned back and grinned. "Just Caleb?"

She smirked. "On our off days, I may even call you Landis."

"Doghouse days?"

She hugged him again. "I doubt there'll be many of those. I love you, Caleb."

"I love you, Kate, more than anything on earth."

"Tia is going to be so happy."

He grinned. "She already knows."

"My goodness! She's wonderful at keeping secrets." She playfully smacked his chest. "Then again, so are you."

He blushed. How endearing! "We bribed Tia with a new doll and a carriage ride."

"I see that." Kate laughed elatedly.

"So, your answer, Princess Dalton?"

"Yes! Of course I will marry you. However, we will not, I repeat not, have a wedding with any kind of mask or costume. That will be a symbol to ourselves and our friends that we'll always have courage to show our true colors."

Caleb chuckled and peeled off the mask of his wife-to-be, then took off his hat and set her mask inside it.

A perfect fit. Like the two of them.

"Agreed. No masks allowed at our wedding."

An ornery look came over her. "And you will let me use your power tools at will."

He grinned. "We can negotiate that one later. But suffice it to say, I'll probably be easily bribed." His gaze raked her mouth so boldly it made her blush.

"You never cease to surprise me, Casanova."

He leaned in and kissed her cheek. "Not Casanova. Or bandit. Or BB. Just Caleb."

She paused and sidled his face in her hands. "You'll never be just Caleb to me. In fact, you never were. You weren't the only one wearing a mask all this time, Caleb. I've been interested from the start."

"Well, let's take that interest to a whole new level— a romantic carriage ride awaits. And I happen to know a little princess who left chocolates and sapphire roses inside."

"From you?"

"From Bri, Tia, Ian, Mitch, Lauren, your parents, Lem. The works. A happy engagement gift of sorts."

"How did they know I'd say yes?"

He smiled. "You've been more transparent lately."

She smiled. "Thanks to you."

"And thanks to you, I'll be the happiest man on earth."

"Unmasked."

He laughed and helped her into the lighted carriage that would begin their engagement season. "Unmasked."

* * * * *

Dear Reader,

Children are amazing to interact with. Book hero Caleb made me laugh many times in this story as he entertained Tia. I loved subjecting him to a princess at a tea party. I'm surrounded by real men who'd do just as Caleb, ignore their egos for the sake of bringing joy to a child. I have pictures on my reader-centric Facebook page of the elaborate paper tea set Caleb made with Tia. I found a wonderful craft link that describes each step with photos, http://spoonful.com/crafts/pretty-paper-teapots. If you have a little girl in your life, she'll adore the homemade tea set but more so, she'll remember the time you spend with her.

Also, here's a link containing photos and instructions to create the healthy veggie scooter snacks Kate made with Tia: www.tasteofhome.com/Recipes/Scooter-Snacks.

I hang out on my Facebook page daily (www.facebook.com/CherylWyattAuthor). I hope you will visit (and "Like") my page for story extras, glimpses, photos and links that bring books alive. Come join my fun community of readers there. I seek reader input often and use reader-generated ideas in books, which makes the process incredibly fun for me.

You are appreciated and loved, prayed for and never, ever, not for one word, noun, page or verb, taken for granted. If you like my books, please tell your friends about them. I cherish readers staying in touch. You mean so much to me (cheryl@cherylwyatt.com).

Blessings to you and your loved ones.

Cheryl Wyatt

Questions for Discussion

1. Caleb was deeply affected by words spoken over him as a child. What words and which person had the most impact (healthy or harmful) over you growing up? Please discuss.

2. Do you think Caleb was wrong to follow his sister's advice to keep up the bandit charade for as long as he did? Why or why not?

3. If you and a date or friend received an invitation to Lem's storybook ball, which character would you and your date/friend show up as?

4. What do you think most contributed to the breakdown of Kate's parents' marriage, and what do you think the turning point was for them in terms of reconciling?

5. Do you hope Asher Stone follows through on his promise to move to Eagle Point? If so, would you enjoy seeing him have his own happily ever after in a future book?

6. Kate was concerned about comrade Dr. Clara Lockhart. Do you think Kate was right to defend Clara's secretiveness surrounding the personal tragedy that brought her to Eagle Point? Please discuss.

7. After Kate had her epiphany about realizing that it was okay if people saw her struggle, what conver-

sation would you imagine Kate would have once Dr. Lockhart returned to work? Do you think Kate would encourage her to open up? If so, how?

8. Caleb was afraid to pray because he felt as though when he did, things got worse. Have you ever experienced this yourself? In what way, and how did you respond?

9. What was your favorite scene and why?

10. Which secondary character(s) would you like to have their own story?

11. Could you understand Caleb's rift with God? How do you think you would have responded in his situation? What advice would you give to someone dealing with similar disappointments?

12. Which character did you relate to most and why?

13. Could you understand the pressure Kate was under to appear strong all the time? If so, how so? Is there anyone in your life who seems to do everything perfectly? How do you think he or she deals with the expectations?

14. Why do you think it took Kate so long to realize who the bandit was? Did you expect her reaction when she found out? Or did you envision a different reaction from her? If so, what did you envision?

15. When you interact with children in your life, what

positive words of affirmation would you speak over them that could have an impact on who they are for the remainder of their lives?

REQUEST YOUR FREE BOOKS!

2 FREE INSPIRATIONAL NOVELS
PLUS 2
FREE
MYSTERY GIFTS

Love Inspired®

YES! Please send me 2 FREE Love Inspired® novels and my 2 FREE mystery gifts (gifts are worth about $10). After receiving them, if I don't wish to receive any more books, I can return the shipping statement marked "cancel." If I don't cancel, I will receive 6 brand-new novels every month and be billed just $4.74 per book in the U.S. or $5.24 per book in Canada. That's a saving of at least 21% off the cover price. It's quite a bargain! Shipping and handling is just 50¢ per book in the U.S. and 75¢ per book in Canada.* I understand that accepting the 2 free books and gifts places me under no obligation to buy anything. I can always return a shipment and cancel at any time. Even if I never buy another book, the two free books and gifts are mine to keep forever.

105/305 IDN F47Y

Name	(PLEASE PRINT)	
Address		Apt. #
City	State/Prov.	Zip/Postal Code

Signature (if under 18, a parent or guardian must sign)

Mail to the Harlequin® Reader Service:
IN U.S.A.: P.O. Box 1867, Buffalo, NY 14240-1867
IN CANADA: P.O. Box 609, Fort Erie, Ontario L2A 5X3

**Are you a subscriber to Love Inspired books
and want to receive the larger-print edition?**
Call 1-800-873-8635 or visit www.ReaderService.com.

* Terms and prices subject to change without notice. Prices do not include applicable taxes. Sales tax applicable in N.Y. Canadian residents will be charged applicable taxes. Offer not valid in Quebec. This offer is limited to one order per household. Not valid for current subscribers to Love Inspired books. All orders subject to credit approval. Credit or debit balances in a customer's account(s) may be offset by any other outstanding balance owed by or to the customer. Please allow 4 to 6 weeks for delivery. Offer available while quantities last.

Your Privacy—The Harlequin® Reader Service is committed to protecting your privacy. Our Privacy Policy is available online at www.ReaderService.com or upon request from the Harlequin Reader Service.

We make a portion of our mailing list available to reputable third parties that offer products we believe may interest you. If you prefer that we not exchange your name with third parties, or if you wish to clarify or modify your communication preferences, please visit us at www.ReaderService.com/consumerchoice or write to us at Harlequin Reader Service Preference Service, P.O. Box 9062, Buffalo, NY 14269. Include your complete name and address.

LI13R

Christmas has a way of reminding us of what really matters—and what could be more important than our loved ones? From husbands and wives to boyfriends and girlfriends to long-lost loves, the real-life romances in this book are surrounded by the joy and blessings of the Christmas season.

Featuring stories by favorite Love Inspired authors, this collection will warm your heart and soothe your soul through the long winter. *A Kiss Under the Mistletoe* beautifully celebrates the way love and faith can transform a cold day in December into the most magical day of the year.

On sale October 29!

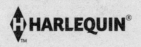